THAT's WHAT WHAT FRIENDS ARE FOR

Ronald
Kidd

ELSEVIER/NELSON BOOKS
New York

Library of Congress Cataloging in Publication Data

Kidd, Ronald.
 That's what friends are for.

 SUMMARY: Two inseparable thirteen-year-old friends confront death when one's illness is diagnosed as leukemia.
 [1. Death—Fiction. 2. Leukemia—Fiction.
 3. Friendship—Fiction] I. Title.
 PZ7.K5315Th   [Fic]   78-14255
 ISBN 0-525-66614-1

Published in the United States by Elsevier/Nelson Books, a division of Elsevier-Dutton Publishing Company, Inc., New York. Published simultaneously in Don Mills, Ontario, by Thomas Nelson and Sons (Canada) Limited.
Printed in the U.S.A.

10 9 8 7 6 5 4 3 2

THAT's WHAT WHAT FRIENDS ARE FOR

Prologue

Something's been bothering me. It's been bothering me for a whole year. I thought maybe it would help to talk about it.

I used to know this guy named Scott. We were in the eighth grade last year. Scott was my best friend. We used to play chess all the time. That's not all we did, of course. As I said, we were best friends. We'd do homework together, too. I'd help him with English, and he'd help me with science and math. It worked out pretty well. Also, he used to play folk-music records for me. The first time I heard Woody Guthrie and the Dillards and Doc Watson was at Scott's house. He really loved the stuff. He'd tap his foot and sort of hum along. I say "sort of" because he couldn't carry a tune for the life of him. The records were good, though. I used to enjoy listening to records with Scott. I used to enjoy doing lots of things with Scott. But Scott died.

I'd never known anybody before who died. No, actually that's not true. My grandmother died when I was four. But I didn't really understand what was going on. My mom and dad told me things like "Your grandmother's gone to heaven" and "We won't be seeing her again, but she's in a happy place." It was as if she just disappeared one day. With Scott it was different. I saw him when he was sick at home, and I saw him in the hospital when he was feeling terrible, and then I saw him lying in his casket at the funeral. I saw the whole thing. No one can tell me that he went to heaven or that he went to a happy place, because I saw where he went. He went into the ground in a wooden box.

It makes me feel rotten to think of Scott in that wooden box. I know it's not my fault or anything. But it just doesn't seem fair for him to be down there and for me to be up here. Especially after how I acted. See, that's what's bothering me. I was a great friend as long as Scott was feeling well, but when he started getting really sick, I didn't want to be around him. I went to visit him a couple of times, but I just couldn't stand seeing him that way. So I just stopped going. Some friend. More like a coward.

I never wanted to talk about this very much. But I've been holding it inside of me for a whole year now. I just can't do it anymore. I have to tell someone. And don't just pat me on the shoulder and say that what I did was okay. It wasn't. I'm not asking you to forgive me. All I'm asking is for you to listen. I have to tell someone.

[1]

If
you didn't know Scott very well, you'd probably think he
was a bully. He was big, especially for somebody twelve
years old. It wasn't just that he had long legs. Scott was big
all over—his chest, his arms, his neck, even his head. He
was as thick and solid as a tree trunk. When he walked, he
rumbled along like a truck. His shoulders would sway
from side to side, and you could just picture him shoving
people out of his way, like bullies do.

Besides looking like a bully, he had the voice of a bully,
gruff and almost mean-sounding. He liked to argue, and
the more excited he got, the louder his voice got. His face
and neck would get red, and he'd pound his fist into his
hand and say things like "You idiot! You don't even know
what you're talking about." Every once in a while, he
would tease people and pretend to threaten them, just to
see if he could scare them. He usually could. Most people

took his threats seriously. They probably thought he was just a big, loud bully.

But once you got to know Scott, you could see that he wasn't really like that. He didn't like to fight, for instance. All he would do in a fight was sit on you. He couldn't stand violence. When we played football in gym class, the coach would always make Scott be a lineman. Scott used to dread that.

Up close, Scott didn't look so mean after all. He had what I'd call a soft face. He had some freckles across his nose, and his eyes were friendly. They were brown, I think. His hands were soft, too. The fingers were fat and blunt. I remember watching him write. He would cradle the pencil in his hand and move it inch by inch across the paper. He poked his tongue out of the corner of his mouth when he was writing. I guess it meant he was trying hard.

If you saw Scott in science class, you'd know for sure he wasn't a bully. He was too smart. He always seemed to know just what the teacher was talking about. Sometimes if the teacher needed an assistant, he'd ask Scott to help him. My personal opinion was that Scott was a better teacher than the teacher. When Scott explained something, you knew just what he meant. If I didn't understand something in class, I never worried about it too much. I'd just ask Scott about it later. He'd straighten me right out.

Actually, that's how we met—in science class. Both of us were just starting seventh grade at this junior high school in Los Angeles. At our school, they called the first half of the seventh grade B7. We were B7s. The sound of that word makes me shiver. It reminds me of all the scare stories we used to hear. There were rumors about the terrible things that happened to B7s—like getting beaten up on the way home from school, or locked in the girls' bathroom. The worst rumor was the one about getting pantsed. That meant that some A9s would gang up on you at school and take your pants off. Then they'd run away and leave you standing there with no pants, right in the middle of campus. The rumor used to scare me to death. I figured one way to protect myself was to get a big friend. So when Scott sat down next to me the first day in science class, I decided we'd be friends. I was hoping he was a nice guy.

"Hi," I ventured. "My name's Gary."

Scott glanced at me. "I'm Scott," he said in his gruff voice, and pulled an issue of *Scientific American* out of his notebook. He opened it and started reading.

I was determined to make friends with him. "What are you reading?" I asked.

"It's an article about the moon."

"Does it say anything about people getting to visit it someday? I mean ordinary people."

Scott looked up from the magazine. He had an irritated expression on his face.

"It mentions the subject," he said, and went back to his reading.

I was feeling brave. "I've always wondered what it would be like up there. With all those craters and things. Do you think I'll ever get to go?"

Scott turned slowly to look at me. He just stared at me for a second. I fidgeted in my seat and wondered whether getting beaten up was worse than getting pantsed.

"Hey, look," I said, "I didn't mean to interrupt you. It's just that I've always been interested in the moon. Maybe after you finish the article, we could talk about it."

He grunted and opened up the magazine again. About

that time the teacher got up from his desk in the front of the room and introduced himself. I decided to wait until after class to talk about the moon.

Science was pretty dull that first day. The teacher spent most of the period having us fill out roll cards and forms. I noticed that in between forms, Scott got time to finish his article. When the bell rang, I was all set to have another try at him, but the teacher asked me to stay after class for a minute to alphabetize the roll cards. By the time I was finished, everyone had gone.

It was noon, so I went down to my locker to get my lunch. Just as I was closing the locker, I heard a voice behind me.

"Do you still want to talk about the moon?" Scott was standing there with his notebook in one hand and a sack lunch in the other. I was pretty surprised.

"Sure," I said. "Let's have lunch together." I figured I'd be safe from getting pantsed for at least one day.

We walked into the lunch area and looked around. It was a big open space, outdoors, with rows of benches and tables. There was an empty bench nearby, so we sat down.

Scott dug into his lunch bag and started pulling things out. It reminded me of the clowns at the circus. You've probably seen that act. A little teeny VW drives out into the ring, and clowns start coming out the door. The funny part is that they just keep coming and coming, more and more of them. That's the way it was with Scott's lunch. He just kept pulling things out—sandwiches, potato chips, pretzels, oranges, bananas, dried figs, cookies, pieces of cake, Mars bars. It was all in that little bag. I couldn't believe it.

"That's some lunch you've got," I said.

"Yeah, I like to eat."

"Eating's not the word for it. You must be like a garbage disposal."

He looked at me, and suddenly I remembered I was talking to somebody twice my size. I started to apologize, but before I could, he began to laugh and slap his leg.

"A garbage disposal," he said in between slaps. "Hey, that's pretty good."

I started laughing, too, probably because I was so relieved. We both laughed pretty hard. It seemed to break the ice between us.

"What elementary school did you go to?" he asked, peeling an orange.

"Winnetka. How about you?"

"Hart Street. I sure got tired of that place. Everybody was so little."

"I'm not exactly Wilt Chamberlain," I pointed out. At the time, I was about four foot eight.

"Hey, look, I don't mind short people," he said. "It's just I don't like everybody short. It makes you feel like a freak."

"It didn't make me feel like a freak," I replied. "I was just getting to like it. There were actually people shorter than me. But now look. I'm a runt again. I have B7 written all over me. First thing you know, somebody's going to pants me."

"Just let them try," Scott said. That made me feel pretty good. Then, out of the blue, he said, "Hey, do you like chess?"

"Sure. I was the Winnetka champion."

"I was the Hart Street champion."

I took a bite out of my peanut-butter sandwich. "Let's play a game sometime," I suggested.

"How about right now?" He pulled a little fold-up chess set out of his notebook and set it up on the bench. I started to get a little worried. Fifteen minutes later, I was even more worried. He had me in checkmate.

"I demand a rematch," I protested, as the bell rang to end lunch period.

Scott crumpled his paper bag and gathered up his books. "Let's play again tomorrow."

"Do you want to have lunch together, too?" I asked.

He nodded. Then he turned and moved off toward his next class. He sure didn't look like a B7. Which was fine with me.

[2]

Eating lunch together after science class got to be a regular thing with Scott and me. As I got to know him, I started to realize that his tough-guy image was just an act. It's true that he was loud, and he did call people idiots and stupid jerks, but underneath it all he could be pretty sensitive sometimes. Take that first day, for instance. I think he knew he had overdone the mean act in science class, and that's why he came up to me afterward and wanted to talk.

Since Scott and I were both B7s and new to the school, it was nice having somebody to eat lunch with. We'd usually play chess, and I'd watch Scott pull things out of his lunch bag. One day he told me about another hobby of his. We had just finished a game of chess. (I won.)

"Do you ever watch people?" he asked.

"I guess so. What do you mean?"

"I mean do you ever just sit and watch people? Right here in the lunch area, for instance."

I looked around. There didn't seem to be much to look at. I turned to Scott and shrugged my shoulders.

He pointed to a row of tables across the lunch area. "Did you ever notice how people sit in the same groups every day? Take the jocks, for instance. They eat over there. See all those guys with letters on their sweaters? That's them. Now why would any idiot want to wear sweaters all the time? It looks ridiculous."

"Maybe it's so that everybody will know that they're sports stars. That's my theory, anyway."

Scott snorted. "My theory is they're stupid.

"Now look over there," he went on. "That group's the brains. You can tell them by their glasses." He was right. At one table almost everyone was wearing glasses. "Another way you can spot them is that lots of the girls have frizzy hair, and the guys like to button their shirts all the way up to the collar. Mainly, they're ugly."

"Wait a minute," I said, smoothing my hair. "There's plenty of smart people who aren't ugly."

"Yeah, but then they wouldn't be brains. See, it's not that the brains are so much smarter than the other good students like, say, you and me. It's just that their brains are the only thing they've got."

I pointed over to another group. They were talking loud and shaking hands a lot. "Who do you think those people are?"

"Campus politicians. See that guy who's always smiling? The one with the striped shirt? He's the student-body president. Most of those other people are student-body officers."

"How do you know all this? You're as new here as I am."

Scott grinned in satisfaction. "I just keep my eyes open. It's called people watching. It's one of my favorite hobbies."

I looked back at the campus politicians. "Do you have to hold an office to be in that group?"

"It helps. But mostly you just have to have a big mouth and smile a lot.

"Don't get me wrong, though," he added quickly. "I like politics—just not their kind of politics. I go for the big issues—peace, democracy, civil rights, equality, things like that. The little details are a waste of time. I don't care about the theme of the school dance or what color we should paint the trash cans."

Of all the other groups Scott pointed out to me, the one I remember best was the bikers. They didn't have choppers or anything like that, of course, because they weren't sixteen yet. But they were going to be ready when the time came. They always wore dirty jeans with oil stains on them. Their hair was long and stringy. The girls wore lots of makeup. Some of them used so much eye makeup that they looked as if they had black eyes. One thing I have to admit, though. Lots of them were well built. When the teachers weren't watching, the guys would put one arm around their girl friends.

During lunch, the teachers used to patrol the area and make sure no one was breaking any rules. On the surface that sounds like a good idea. If people get into a fight or throw paper on the ground, then the teachers stop them. Great. But it didn't usually work that way. The reason it didn't was that they spent all their time enforcing three dumb rules.

The first rule was that you couldn't hold hands or make out. In my opinion, that rule was a joke. I'm not saying they should have encouraged that sort of thing.

I'm just saying people like the bikers were going to hold hands and make out no matter what you did. Scott used to say it was the same with prostitution. People were going to do it no matter what the rules were, so you might as well make it legal and get it out into the open. I guess I agree with him. I always enjoyed watching the bikers make out, anyway.

The second rule was that you weren't allowed to eat standing up. When Scott and I heard that, we cracked up. I mean, it was totally ridiculous. But it was even more ridiculous to watch people try and get around it. No matter what rule you make, some people are going to stretch it as far as they can. So the big thing in our school was eating while you leaned against a railing or a table. That way, one part of you was in contact with something, and it was kind of borderline about whether you were sitting down or not. Some teachers let you get away with it, others didn't.

The third rule was about book covers. The teachers used to make us put paper book covers on our textbooks to protect them. At lunch, if a teacher saw you with a book that didn't have a cover, he'd take it. For some reason, Scott used to avoid getting book covers. If he got in a jam, he'd borrow one of mine. The trouble was, one of the teachers caught on to Scott's game. This one teacher was a real nut on book covers. When it was his turn to patrol the lunch area, he'd really zero in on book covers. He didn't care about any of the other rules, just as long as you had book covers. If you didn't, he'd take the book, and you'd have to go pick it up at his office. Whenever you saw him, he always had a big pile of books that he was carrying around with him. Everybody used to call him the Bald-Headed Book Snatcher. Well, he spotted Scott right away. It really made Scott mad. Every time he looked up, there was the Bald-Headed Book Snatcher. Scott used to spend a lot of time going to his office and picking up books.

The reason I mention these three rules is that I think it shows something about adults—parents and teachers especially. I think that adults spend too much time worrying about the way things should be. They have an idea in their mind about the way you should dress or the way you should talk or the way you should act at lunch. Then they try to make everything just the way they want it, even if it doesn't make any sense. Why shouldn't you be able to eat standing up? Name one good reason.

Who made up these rules, anyway? Who said you can't tell somebody that he is dying? If you ask me, I think a person should be able to do or say whatever's on his mind, as long as it doesn't hurt somebody. I think when a person spends all his time worrying about whether he's going to break a rule or hurt somebody's feelings, sometimes he never gets around to saying what's on his mind. And then first thing you know, he's lost his chance. It's too late to say anything, because there's no one left to listen.

[3]

The first time I went over to Scott's house, I still didn't know him too well. At that time we'd only had lunch together once or twice. I still had this basic idea that Scott was mostly a big guy who would protect me from getting pantsed.

Like I told you, Scott sometimes acted like a bully and talked loud, so I half expected his mom and dad to be big and loud, too. I couldn't believe it when I met them. They were really nice, and both of them were short.

I came to find out that Mrs. Lewis was friendly to everybody. She was always doing things for people. For instance, she was active in the PTA and used to take a booth at the school fair. I won a goldfish from her once. She also used to be a member of different Quaker groups. Whenever there was a fire or a natural disaster somewhere, she'd do volunteer work with the Quaker groups collecting food and clothes. Mr. and Mrs. Lewis weren't Quakers or anything. In fact, Mr. Lewis was Jewish. Mrs. Lewis was some other religion. But she sometimes said that her religion was people.

Mr. Lewis was nice, too. He was interested in everything, especially political issues. That first time I met him, I barely had time to tell him my name before he asked me what I thought of affirmative action. Whenever he got onto politics or some other topic he really liked, his eyes would get shiny, and he'd slide down in his favorite chair and get into his talking position. That meant his head was halfway down the back of the chair and he was sort of sitting on his back, if you can picture what I'm saying. I've seen lots of kids do that, but there aren't too many grown-ups who do. Most of them talk about good posture and try to sit up straight themselves. Mr. Lewis was different that way. He'd slump down in his talking position and put his fingertips together. Then he'd talk in kind of a soft, far-off voice about pollution or civil rights or getting rid of the death penalty. I suppose that's where Scott got some of his ideas.

Anyway, after Scott had introduced me to his mom and dad that first day, he said to come on back to his room. I figured he wanted to play chess. When we got back there, Scott closed the door and turned to me.

"Have you ever seen *Playboy* magazine?" he asked.

"Sure," I said, trying to make it sound as if I read it every day. Actually, I'd only looked at it twice, once at the barber shop and once at a newsstand, and both times I'd been so nervous about somebody catching me that I didn't see much.

"I've got a whole bunch of them here," he said, pulling them out from under his bed.

"Wow, where did you get them?"

"From my mom and dad's room. Dad subscribes and keeps them on a stack next to the bed."

"He subscribes? To *Playboy* magazine? Are you kidding?"

"No, I'm not kidding. He says it has good stories and articles in it." A little grin flashed across Scott's face. "But I've noticed that's not the first thing he turns to." Scott opened the top magazine to the middle and folded out a page. "Here's where he always turns first."

"What does your mom think about *Playboy?*"

"She doesn't mind. She says it's just another magazine, and that looking at all kinds of people is natural."

I started to ask Scott why he had closed the door, but I decided not to. Instead, I took one of the magazines and started looking through it. There were plenty of pictures in it. I was looking at one, and suddenly something occurred to me.

"Hey, Scott, you know what? I kept thinking these ladies remind me of something, but I couldn't think what it was. Now I know. It's the bikers' girlfriends. Lots of the ladies in these pictures are built the same and have the same expression on their faces."

Scott glanced over my shoulder. "Wow, you're right. Put jeans and a leather jacket on that one, and you'd never be able to tell the difference. I bet we'll see some of those bikers' girls in *Playboy* in a few years."

He went back to his magazine, and I tried to picture some of those girls at school posing for a *Playboy* picture. It was kind of interesting. I felt a little funny thinking about it, but mostly I enjoyed it.

Scott's house was the kind of place where you could just go and relax. After that first visit, I got in the habit of stopping by most days after school. Scott's mom would fix us some lemonade or a snack of some kind, and then we'd go back to his room. But don't get the idea that all we ever did was look at *Playboy*. We did that some of the time, but lots of times we'd study, too.

First we'd do our math and science. Scott would whip right through his and then help me out on the parts I was having trouble with. It wasn't like cheating, though. Scott was careful about that. He didn't like to cheat. He wouldn't just give me the answers. We'd go through, say, a math problem I didn't understand. I'd tell him what I thought I should do on the problem. Then he'd ask me questions, just like the teacher would do. By answering the questions, I'd usually be able to figure out the problem. I learned a lot of math and science that way.

After math and science, we'd do our English. That was my department. I've always been good at English. I'm not sure why, but spelling came easy. Also, I liked to read. That helped in English class. Usually for homework we'd have a story to read and then questions to answer about it. Scott enjoyed most of the stories, but he hated answering those questions. I have to admit, some of them were dumb. Scott would read a question and then slam the book closed. He'd yell something like "How should I know what the author was trying to say? What a stupid question. He just wrote a story, that's all." The questions asked about things like symbols and hidden meanings. I used to try to explain to Scott that it was a game English teachers play. You just had to play along with them. Actually, I sort of enjoyed it. I got pretty good at making up wild answers. The wilder the answers were, the more the teachers seemed to like it. But Scott didn't like it. If something wasn't written down in black and white, he didn't want to waste his time on it. He would rather do a math problem, because there was a right answer and a wrong answer. None of this opinion stuff.

One day after we'd finished our homework, Scott said he wanted me to hear something. He went over to his bookshelf, where he had a bunch of records. I'd never really noticed them before. He pulled one out and showed it to me. It was a Woody Guthrie album.

"Have you ever heard of this guy?" he asked.

"Isn't he a folk singer? Sort of like Peter, Paul, and Mary?"

Scott exploded. "Peter, Paul, and Mary? You shouldn't even mention them in the same breath with Woody Guthrie. He was a real folk singer, not one of these plastic types. He was one of the people."

"What people?"

"*The* people, dummy. Just plain, simple people, like you and me. Nothing fancy. Here, listen to this." He pulled the record out of the jacket and put it on his portable record player. When the music started, there were all sorts of scratching and crackling noises behind it. He must have played that record a lot.

The song was called "Talking Dust Bowl." It was about a farmer in Oklahoma who had to sell his farm because of the dust storms. Woody Guthrie played a guitar and just kind of talked the words. At first I didn't see what was so great about it, but the longer the song went on, the more I enjoyed it. It almost seemed that the farmer was right there talking to you.

When the song was over, Scott reached down to the record player and picked the arm up. "Pretty good, huh?"

"Yeah, I really liked it. I'd like to hear him in person sometime."

"You can't. He's dead. He died of a rare disease called

Huntington's chorea. It was really sad, because it took him about ten years to die. He just kept getting worse and worse. He couldn't even write songs a lot of the time, because he was too sick."

Scott put the arm back down on the record, and we listened some more. There was a song called "Cumberland Gap" and another one called "Chain Gang Special." All the songs had that same scratchy sound. After a while it just seemed like part of the music.

Next he played some records by Doc Watson, who was a blind violinist (Scott said fiddler). Then he played some Pete Seeger and some Dillards songs.

I enjoyed all the music, but not the same way Scott did. He would tap his foot and thump his fingers on his knee and hum along off key. He really got carried away. It was interesting about Scott and folk music. You wouldn't think a guy who liked science experiments and math problems would go for music about farmers and chain gangs and drinking whiskey on Saturday night. But it was just about Scott's favorite thing. He even took up playing the guitar. You should have seen him trying to press down the right strings with his huge fingers. Half of the time he'd press down two at once and mess up the chord. It should have been funny, but when Scott was poking his tongue out of the corner of his mouth and concentrating, I could never laugh at him.

All in all, I guess if I had to pick out one thing that reminds me most of Scott, it would be folk music. Every time I hear it, I think about those afternoons at his house doing homework and looking at *Playboy* and listening to records.

[4]

Scott and I spent most of our time over at his house. We didn't go to my house very much. Mom used to ask me why I didn't invite my friends over more, and I usually just said I didn't know. Then she'd get this sad look on her face and stare at the floor for a while. My mom's like that. She gets her feelings hurt pretty easily. I guess you could say in some ways she's like a little kid. She even looks like a little kid. She's small, like me. When I was in elementary school, I remember going to the children's room of the public library and sitting in those miniature chairs they have. Mom used to sit in them, too, and she'd fit just fine. For once, her feet would touch the floor.

Anyway, whenever Mom mentioned anything about inviting friends over, I'd feel kind of bad. So one Saturday I decided to make up for it by inviting Scott over for the whole day. When I told Mom about it, she got really excited and said she'd make some grilled-cheese sandwiches for lunch.

Scott knocked at the door about ten o'clock. He was wearing a T-shirt and jeans and had a *Scientific American* in his hand.

"What's that for?" I asked, letting him in. "Afraid you'll get bored?" I was just kidding, of course.

"Nope. I just like to keep one of these with me. You never know when you'll get a few minutes to read."

As we walked into the living room, Mom came out of the kitchen. "Hi, Scott," she said with a bright grin on her face. "We haven't seen you for such a long time. We've really missed you. We just want you to know that you're always welcome."

"Uh—thanks," Scott replied. He looked at me as if he didn't know what to say next.

"I've got the chessboard all set up in my room," I said. "How about a game?"

We went back and sprawled on the carpet next to the board. As the game developed, it turned into one of our typical matches. What I mean by that is that Scott would look at the board and in maybe half a minute he'd make his move. I was always a perfectionist, so I'd take four or five minutes. By the time I moved, he'd already decided on *his* next move, so right away he'd go ahead and make it. Now here I was back where I started. Pretty soon I'd begin to feel bad about taking so much time. The funny thing was, I'd get so worried about it that I couldn't concentrate, so I'd take even longer. About that time, Scott would start thumping his fingers on the floor. That's what I mean by a typical match. I'd worry a lot, and Scott would thump his fingers a lot.

We played two games, and Scott won both of them. I

guess his thumping was bothering me that day. We were on our third game when Mom called us to lunch.

We went into the dining room and sat down at the table. Mom and Dad were already there. Mom had put a grilled-cheese sandwich and some potato chips on everybody's plate. She had made milk shakes for Scott and me. Actually, they weren't real milk shakes. She just called them that. They were instant breakfast and milk. Mom was drinking iced tea. Dad was having a beer.

I guess I haven't mentioned my dad up to now. I suppose that's no accident. Dad and I aren't that close. It's always seemed that he wanted me to be something I'm not. I think he'd have liked me to be tall, handsome, and athletic—in other words, like him. But I'm not. I'm short, plain, and uncoordinated.

Dad wanted me to be a star baseball player. He signed me up for Little League when I was ten, and he was out there at every game, yelling advice at the top of his lungs. It made me nervous. Once when I was playing right field, I let a ball roll between my legs. By the time I chased it down I was so nervous that I accidentally threw up on the ball. Then I couldn't decide whether to pick it up or leave it there. Finally I threw it in. They just let it roll. That was the last year I played Little League.

I guess Dad had been watching football in the den, because that's what he started talking about when we sat down to lunch. He took a drink of his beer and turned to Scott.

"Oklahoma's sure got a powerful team this year. Think they'll beat Nebraska?"

"I don't really know, Mr. Matthews," Scott replied. "I don't follow football very much."

"Are you kidding?" said Dad. "A big guy like you? How much do you weigh?"

Scott squirmed in his seat. "Around one eighty. But—"

"That's fantastic," said Dad. "By the time you're in high school, you'll be up around two hundred for sure. You're a natural-born tackle. If Gary were that size, I'd have him working out with a blocking dummy every afternoon."

"Mr. Matthews, I'm really not that athletic. And mainly it just doesn't interest me. I like science."

"Oh," said Dad. He glanced over at me and then took another drink of beer. I could tell he wanted to say something, but he didn't because Mom was starting to fidget.

"How did your chess game go, boys? she asked.

"Pretty good," I said quickly. I usually tried to help her out when she changed the subject. "Scott beat me twice, but I was ahead in the third game."

"You were?" asked Scott. "I couldn't tell who was ahead, with you taking so long to move."

"How are your parents, Scott?" Mom asked all of a sudden.

"Huh? Oh, they're okay, I guess."

"I'm so fond of your mother," Mom said. "I think she's just the sweetest person."

"She makes good tuna-fish sandwiches, that's for sure," Scott replied. I think he was serious. Tuna-fish sandwiches were pretty important to Scott.

After lunch my dad pushed his chair back from the table. "Okay, guys," he said in this jock voice he liked to use, "how about a game of catch in the backyard?"

Scott looked over at me. I shrugged.

"Sure," I said to Dad. I figured we could just do it for a few minutes to pacify him.

Dad got a softball from the garage, and we went out in back.

"You guys stand over there next to each other," he directed, "and I'll stand over here and throw some to you."

He lobbed the ball to me first. I managed to catch it and throw it back to him without dropping it. Then he threw it to Scott. Scott wasn't too good in sports. He had a tough time making his body do what he wanted it to do. When he tried to catch the ball, he kind of lunged at it with his arms stuck straight out in front of him. The ball bounced off his hands as if they were made of United States Steel. Scott picked it up quickly and slung it back to Dad. It hit the ground about halfway there and rolled to a stop at his feet. Dad just stood there and looked at it for a minute. Then he picked it up and threw it back to me, a little harder this time. I bobbled it a little bit but still caught it and lobbed it back. He threw it harder to Scott, too, and Scott dropped it again. Nobody was saying anything. Dad just kept throwing the ball to us, harder and harder. Pretty soon it started stinging when it hit our hands. We didn't catch many of them, but that didn't stop Dad. It was as if he were in a trance or something. Then, one of his really fast ones went through Scott's hands and hit him in the stomach. It knocked the wind out of him, and he doubled over. That seemed to snap Dad out of it. He rushed over to Scott with a worried look on his face. It was almost a scared look.

"You okay, Scott?" He gripped Scott's shoulder. Scott couldn't talk for a minute, because the wind was knocked out of him. "Hey, Scott, you okay?" Dad kept asking. Finally, Scott nodded and straightened up. Dad let out his breath, as if he'd been the one who had been hit in the stomach.

"Let's go back inside," he said.

Scott didn't stay too much longer that day. And after that, we spent even less time at my house and more time at Scott's. It seemed to work out better that way.

[5]

When you're twelve years old, one of the main problems you have is getting around. You can walk, but that's pretty tiring, especially when you already have to walk to and from school most days. You can ride your bike, but that only gets you so far. You can have your parents drive you, but if they're busy, then you're out of luck. Or you can take the bus.

I had only been on a bus two or three times in my whole life. Every time, it had been with my parents, usually when the car had broken down. I really enjoyed it. The people were interesting, and sitting up high like that made you feel that you could look down on the whole world. The trouble was, Mom and Dad didn't like for me to ride the bus alone. It scared Mom, and Dad was sure that everybody on it was a pervert. So my parents didn't let me ride the bus.

Scott's parents didn't let him do it, either, so naturally

Scott and I both wanted to go on a bus ride. I wanted to go to Hollywood, and Scott wanted to go to the Museum of Science and Industry. We ended up deciding to do both. We figured that if we allowed a whole Saturday, we could do one thing in the morning and the other in the afternoon.

When the day came, we each told our parents that we would be at the other's house, so they wouldn't suspect anything. Then we met at the bus stop and waited for the nine-thirty bus. It got there right on time. We stepped up inside, and the doors clattered shut behind us.

Scott gave his money to the driver, just like you're supposed to, but when I reached into my pocket, the bus lurched forward and I fell into an old lady.

The bus driver yelled at me, "Hey, watch what you're doing, kid. You might knock somebody over." The lady wasn't hurt, but I felt terrible. I told her I was sorry. When I gave the bus driver my money, he glared at me.

Scott and I went all the way to the very back of the bus. We had the last row to ourselves.

"That driver's a stupid jerk," Scott said, looking up toward the front. "Did he think you fell over on purpose or something?"

"It was his fault anyway," I chimed in, "for starting up all of a sudden like that." I kept my eye on the driver and pretty soon started noticing that he was being grumpy to just about everybody. He made it look like a requirement for the job. He always had to have some complaint. Either you didn't get your money out fast enough or you were standing in the door or you were making too much noise. He'd give you a sour look and then turn back to the road, shaking his head.

I had to admit, though, he was a pretty good driver. He

would go in and out of traffic like someone driving a sports car. It didn't bother him if a car was coming or not. He'd just flick on that turn signal and pull out. If you were in the way, tough luck. He could even drive while he was taking money and handing out transfers. Plenty of times we saw him hand out a transfer, grump at some-body, and pull out into heavy traffic all at the same time.

Most of the people who rode the bus were older ladies. Scott pointed out that you could tell the regulars by the way they acted.

"They've got sort of a routine," he said. "They have just the right change when they get on, and they call the bus driver by his name, Mr. So-and-So. Sometimes he doesn't even grump at them. Then they go straight back to a seat and sit there like it's their favorite chair in front of the TV. If they see a friend, they sit together and talk about all kinds of little things that no one else cares about, like their recipe for chicken casserole. If they don't see a friend, they usually just pull a library book out of their purse and start reading. That's their routine."

Among the passengers there were winos, mothers tak-ing their kids shopping, old men in straw hats, younger men who looked as if they were angry about having to ride on the bus, and weirdos. The weirdos would usually mumble to themselves or laugh out loud for no reason. Every once in a while, a pretty girl would get on the bus, and we'd make up a story about her.

"Look at that one," I whispered when this one pretty girl sat down near us. "I bet she's a princess who got hit on the head and dumped onto a street corner in Reseda and got a job as a secretary because she has amnesia and doesn't even know she's a princess."

"You're crazy," said Scott. "She's part of a gang, and

she's going to Hollywood to check out the floor plan of a big bank they're going to rob. You can tell she's a wanted criminal. It's written all over her face."

Whoever got on the bus, Scott and I would talk about them. It was fun to do, almost better than people watching in the lunch area.

We got off the bus at the corner of Hollywood and Highland, which is Hollywood's main intersection. As we went out the door, Scott yelled back to the bus driver, "Keep up the good work."

We weren't exactly sure what we wanted to see, so we just started walking down Hollywood Boulevard. There were stars' names on the sidewalk, and we read those out loud for a while. We had just gotten to Greta Garbo when this sad-looking guy with baggy pants walked up to us.

"You fellas been saved?" he asked.

"What do you mean, saved?" said Scott.

"I mean, have you found Jesus?"

"Who?"

"Jesus. You know, Jesus."

Scott shrugged his shoulders. "Hey, look, I'm sorry. We're new in town." We walked off. The first store we came to, we ducked inside and burst out laughing. The people in there must have thought we were nuts.

There were some interesting little shops along Hollywood Boulevard, and we started drifting in and out of them to see what they had. One was a used-book store. When we went in, Scott found some old issues of *Scientific American* and started looking through those. I went into the paperbacks and flipped through a few, looking for the dirty parts. It was hard to do, because I had to keep checking the store owner to see if he noticed what I was doing. A minute later, when I was looking through some old *Playboys,* I got so interested in the pictures that I forgot to check the owner. All of a sudden I heard this voice behind me saying real loud, "Come back when you're eighteen, sonny." All the people in the store looked around at me, and some of them laughed. Scott thought it was hilarious. The rest of that day he kept saying, "Come back when you're eighteen, sonny," and laughing loudly and slapping his leg the way he did sometimes. It was pretty embarrassing.

Hollywood had a great ice-cream shop called C. C. Brown's, where we decided to eat lunch. Scott had discovered on the bus that he had a hole in his pocket, so he'd been carrying his change around in his hand. As soon as we sat down, he put the change on the table in front of him. When the waitress came over to clear off the table, she must have thought Scott's money was a tip from the last customer, so she slid it off the table and put it in her pocket.

"Hey, that's my money!" Scott exclaimed.

"Sure, kid," the waitress said in this bored voice. "What do you two want?"

"Hey, I mean it, that's my money," Scott persisted. "There was fifty-three cents there."

"He's telling the truth," I said.

"Look, sonny," she replied, glowering at Scott. "I make half my living on tips, and I'm not about to let you walk off with one. What kind of kid are you, anyway?"

Scott's face was starting to get red. He had a couple of dollars in bills, but I think he was counting on that money for the bus fare home. "I tell you, that's my money. I've got a hole in my pocket. That's why I put the money on the table. Here, look," he said, sliding out of the booth. He pulled his pants pocket inside out and stuck his finger through the hole. "Try it yourself if you want," he offered.

The waitress looked at him funny. "You're a weird kid," she said. "If you want the money that bad, you can have it." She scooped a handful of change from her pocket, counted out fifty-three cents, and put it on the table.

"Now what do you two want?" she asked, looking at me but glancing at Scott every once in a while out of the corner of her eye.

"A tuna-fish sandwich, a Coke, and a hot-fudge sundae," I said.

"Same," mumbled Scott, counting his change.

C. C. Brown's was right next door to Grauman's Chinese Theater, so we went there after lunch. Grauman's Chinese is the place where all the stars put their footprints in the cement. Besides the footprints, there were handprints, too, and other things, like Jimmy Durante's noseprint and Trigger's hoofprints. But the print I remember best was one I'm sure you've never heard of. It said, "Charles Nelson, Talent Contest Winner, 1949." Scott was the one who showed it to me.

"What happened," he explained, "was that some guy was the winner in a talent contest. The prize was to have his footprints put in at Grauman's Chinese. Well, they went through with it all right, but they forgot to mention one thing. Instead of putting his footprints in front with the rest, they stuck them over here at the side, where no one ever looks." He started laughing that loud laugh of his. "What a riot. That stupid idiot actually believed his footprints would be next to Cary Grant's or somebody's."

At first I thought it was funny, too, but later on I decided it was sad. That poor guy probably got his hopes up and told his neighbors and friends all about it. Then when they actually went to see his footprints here they were stuck out by the bushes. It was a rotten thing to do, in my opinion. Sometimes you wonder about people.

After Grauman's Chinese, we took the bus over to the Museum of Science and Industry. All the way over there, Scott kept describing the museum to me. His mom had taken him there once before.

When we got inside, Scott just about went crazy. He loved all those displays and models and gadgets. He'd run from one to another, pushing buttons and watching what would happen. Sometimes a miniature earth would go around the sun. Sometimes there would be a fake earthquake in a little model city. Sometimes the button would start up an engine that had been cut in half so you could see how it ran. I'd usually be two or three steps behind Scott. He'd tell me to hurry up. Then he'd explain to me what each display meant. Part of the time I didn't really care, but mostly he made it interesting.

The museum had a good model-train display, but Scott didn't like it much. He said it was just a crowd pleaser and didn't have much to do with science. Actually, it was my favorite exhibit. It took up a whole room, and it had all kinds of little buildings and trestles and water towers. You could walk across a bridge that went over the exhibit. When you got in the middle, you could look down at the trains and you'd swear you were flying over a real town in an airplane.

While Scott and I were at the train exhibit, two girls came up next to us and started talking about it. They were about our age. They kept saying how much work it must have taken and how marvelous it all was. Then one of them turned to Scott and said they had never seen this exhibit before; did he know anything about it? He said it was the biggest piece of junk in the whole museum. They got this strange look on their faces and walked off. I got really mad at him. There are certain things you just don't do, I told him. All he would say was that those girls were stupid idiots. I told him that might be true, but maybe we could have talked to them for a minute. Actually, I had been all set to explain the whole thing to them and tell them how great it was.

The afternoon kind of lost its zip after that. We stayed a while longer and then got back on the bus and started home. The ride took about an hour. There were probably just as many interesting people on the bus as there had been that morning, but somehow it didn't seem as exciting. Scott and I mostly just sat there and looked out the window.

[6]

Ⓞne
Friday night we were at Scott's house trying to think of
something to do. Scott was anxious to get out of the
house, because he had been sick earlier that week and
had been cooped up inside for so long. It was the second
time he had been absent from school in the two months I
had known him. It struck me odd at the time that such a
huge guy could get sick so easily.

While we were thinking of something to do, we were
listening to Joe Pyne. Joe Pyne had one of those radio
shows where people called in and talked to him. Scott
really liked that show. One reason was that he disagreed
with most of what Joe Pyne said. Whenever Pyne said
something bad about people on welfare or that we should
spend more money on defense, or something like that,
Scott would get really angry. He'd pound his fist into his
palm and say, "Pyne, you idiot!" The other reason Scott
liked the show was because of the callers. A lot of nutty

people called that show. They'd say things like the Martians had landed, or that fluoride in the water was making us sterile. Scott would laugh hard and say something like "What a jerk!" His favorite part of the show was when Joe Pyne would tell somebody off and then hang up on him. Pyne had lots of good lines. One good one was, "Why don't you stick your thumb in your ear and go bowling?" Scott used to save up those lines and talk about using them on people he didn't like.

Anyway, we were listening to Joe Pyne, and a movie commercial came on. The movie was supposed to be about this F.B.I. agent who chases some dope smugglers all around the country.

"Hey, that sounds pretty good," I said. "Want to go see it?"

"Okay," said Scott. "I haven't seen a movie for a while."

We got the movie section of the paper and took it back to his parents' bedroom, where the extension phone was. Scott started calling theaters where the movie was playing. He was in kind of a rowdy mood from listening to Joe Pyne.

The first place he called must have had a recording, because he said, "How's it going, fella?" and then, "I understand your dog got run over." The second theater must have had a woman's voice on the recording, because he said, "Hey, honey, how about a date?" The third time, he decided to try out one of Joe Pyne's lines. "You idiot!" he yelled. "If you had any brains, you'd be dangerous!" Just about that time, his mom walked past the door. You should have seen the look on her face.

He finally found one theater where the movie started at a good time, and he talked his dad into dropping us off there. When we got into the car, I happened to glance over at Scott's dad. I couldn't believe it. He was sitting in his talking position, way down in the seat. I guess he always drove like that. I couldn't figure out how he was going to see over the steering wheel. Scott didn't seem to be worried, though, so I decided not to say anything. I always tried to be polite, and I thought it would be pretty rude to ask Scott's dad how the heck he thought he was going to see the road. Anyway, we got to the show without having any accidents. When Scott's dad drove off, his head was down so low it looked as if the car didn't have a driver.

We bought our tickets and got in line. Scott looked around for a few minutes and then pointed to a couple up ahead of us.

"Ten to one they're on a first date," he said. "You can always spot the ones on a first fate. Look how shiny his shoes are. Look how he has his hands in his pockets, trying to be casual."

"She sure is smiling hard," I remarked.

"Exactly," he said, just the way Sherlock Holmes might say it if Watson had observed something important. "Also, look at the way they keep looking around and smoothing their clothes. It's got to be a first date."

There were a biker and his girl standing in line nearby. He had his arm around her.

"How about them?" I asked. "Think they're on a first date?"

"You can't tell," Scott said. "Bikers are different. They might have just met, maybe down at the bowling alley. Plus, bikers don't shine their shoes or anything, so it's impossible to tell."

The line started moving, and pretty soon we were inside.

"Let's sit in the first row," Scott said, pulling me after him. "It makes everything big and loud."

He was right. When the movie started, the people on the screen looked huge. Sometimes their noses would be bigger than your whole body. Even Scott's whole body. When they were just standing up in a regular position, their feet and legs would be gigantic and then they'd get smaller as you went up. Their heads looked like little croquet balls on top of their giant bodies. It was great. All the music and voices blared out at you, because the speakers were right there behind the screen. You could really get involved in the movie that way.

The movie itself was a real disappointment. We started making funny remarks when we got bored, which turned out to be most of the time. Some of the things we said were so funny that we'd laugh out loud and have trouble stopping. Unfortunately, it tended to happen during quiet scenes.

When we got tired of making funny remarks, we started going out for candy. I made three trips, buying popcorn, a Coke, and a box of Jordan almonds. Scott made five trips altogether, getting a large root beer, a Mars bar, beef jerky, peanuts, and a chocolate-covered banana. We discovered that there's a real art to picking a good time to go and get candy during a movie. You get a feel for it. Scott and I had different theories about it. My theory was that nothing much usually happens for a few minutes after a big scene. That's when I'd go. Scott's theory was to go as soon as they started kissing.

It might sound funny that somebody who enjoyed reading *Playboy* didn't like to watch kissing in movies. Actually, it made sense if you knew Scott. Scott believed in a scientific view of girls. None of this mushy stuff like kissing and nibbling on ears and staring into each other's eyes. That just cluttered things up. He felt that when you were judging girls, you had to step back and look at them from a distance and then figure their good points against their bad points. You couldn't let emotions cloud up the issue.

As part of Scott's scientific view of girls, he made up what we started calling the Big Five. The Big Five was a list of our five favorite girls. It was a nonmushy rating system.

The way we picked the girls depended on two main things. First of all, they had to be good-looking. That usually meant a pretty face and a nice smile. No zits. It also meant a good figure, but in seventh grade not everybody has a good figure. It was okay if they were a little skinny, as long as it looked as if they'd grow out of it. Of course, if they were built or something, that really helped. The other important thing was what kind of personality they had. We liked the quiet types who spoke in soft tones and were always nice to you. We also liked the bubbly types with lots of energy, who were interested in everything. You had to watch that type, though. If a girl was too bubbly, she could get on your nerves.

Every week we'd get together and figure out the Big Five. It was based on what happened that particular week, so it changed a lot. For instance, if Irene Blume hadn't been very friendly that week, she might drop from number one to number three or four. She might not even be ranked. Usually she was, though, because she had the best legs in the whole seventh grade. Or, for instance, if Barbara Birch was grumpy that week, she might not make the list. Then there were always the special cases. Like the time Arlene Katz got a nose job. She still wasn't very good-looking, but there was so much improvement we decided to make her number five for a week. Or the time Janice McMillan, who didn't wear a bra yet but could have used one, kept bending over to pick up her pencil.

That earned her a number two. Cases like that didn't stay on the list for long, though. They'd make a big splash, but a week later they'd be gone. It was the really nice girls who stayed in the Big Five week after week.

[7]

The summer after seventh grade was the summer of Honors Science. Scott and I first found out about it a few weeks before school was out. We were sitting in English class at the time. Mr. Merrick was talking about *The Scarlet Letter*. He had been trying to explain what the *A* on Hester Prynne's blouse stood for. He was pacing back and forth in front of the room, adjusting his glasses and clearing his throat. Just as he was getting into it, an office messenger came in the door with a slip of paper in his hand. For once, Mr. Merrick seemed glad to be interrupted.

He took the note and glanced at it and then said, "Gary and Scott, you're wanted at the office."

Scott and I looked at each other across the room. Getting summoned to the office usually meant trouble. I went up and took the note from Mr. Merrick, and Scott and I went out the door and into the hall.

"What do you think they want, Scott?" My voice was trembling a little bit. "You think we're in trouble?"

Scott's face was kind of chalky. "How could we be in trouble? What did we do wrong?" His voice was even gruffer than usual. It got that way sometimes when he was trying to pretend he wasn't nervous.

"Maybe they're finally going to get you for not putting covers on your books," I said.

"Well, if that was it," he pointed out, "why would they want you to come?"

"I guess that's true," I admitted. "But it must be something. Maybe they deciphered our handwriting on the bathroom walls. Maybe they want us to start washing our gym shorts. Maybe they spotted us standing up while we were eating. Let's face it, we're no angels."

All the way down the hall, I kept naming the things we could be in trouble for. By the time we walked into the office, I was sure that something terrible was going to happen.

The lady at the counter showed us into the office of Mr. Harris, the boys' vice principal. Everybody at school called him Hard Ass Harris. People said that if Hard Ass caught you walking around campus without book covers or while holding hands with a girl in the hall, he could really make life miserable for you.

"Sit down, men," he boomed. He always called us men, not boys. I thought it was kind of dumb. After all, we were only twelve. I didn't have any hair on my chest yet.

Hard Ass looked straight at us. "You two men have been chosen out of the whole seventh grade for a special assignment." I had heard that Hard Ass used to be a Marine drill sergeant. He had an unusual way of putting things. "Your assignment is Honors Science. It's a special science program at Mission Junior High. Students from all over the valley will be in it—something like an all-star team." He narrowed his eyes and gave us a tight Knute Rockne grin. I had heard somewhere that he wanted to be a football coach.

I let out a sigh of relief and looked over at Scott. He was just staring at Mr. Harris, and his eyes were all shiny. It reminded me of the way his father looked when he got excited over something.

Hard Ass stood up. "Congratulations, men," he said. He shook Scott's hand and then mine. "We'll be filling you in on the game plan as soon as we get more information."

We thanked him and left. When we got into the hall, I started kind of jumping and hopping around.

"Can you believe it, Scott? We're all-stars. Chosen out of the whole seventh grade."

Scott's eyes were still shiny, and he had this little smile on his face. "Yeah," he mumbled. You could almost see the reflection in his eyes of rows and rows of test tubes and Bunsen burners. He must have been planning his experiments already.

Myself, I didn't care that much about experiments. I was just excited about having been chosen, like an all-star. Mostly, though, I was excited about getting out of Hard Ass Harris's office with my body in one piece.

The first day of Honors Science, Scott and I were at Mission Junior High bright and early. The class was supposed to start at nine o'clock and go until twelve, every day for six weeks. It was still only eight thirty, so we had a chance to talk for a few minutes while we waited for the others to arrive.

"I wonder what this teacher's going to be like," I said.

"He'll probably be a professional scientist or something like that," Scott replied. "They don't mess around in these Honors classes. Maybe he's from Cal Tech or UCLA, and they made special arrangements for him to teach this class. Anyway, I bet he'll be a real pro."

"Excuse me, please," said a voice. Scott was standing in front of the classroom door, and somebody wanted to get by. It was an older man with wrinkled clothes, probably the janitor. Scott moved to the side, and the guy let himself into the room. He propped open the door and started straightening the desks and chairs.

Scott spoke through the doorway. "Pardon me, but a class will be starting in here at nine."

"Yes, I know," the man said.

Scott persisted. "What I mean is, we'll need the room pretty soon."

"So will I," replied the man, scooting a chair across the floor. He looked up at us from across the room and smiled. "I'm the teacher."

Scott turned to me with an expression of horror on his face. I didn't know what to say. Finally I shrugged and suggested, "Why don't we go in?"

I walked through the door, and Scott stumbled in behind me. We put our notebooks on a couple of desks in the front row. Scott sat down and stared glumly at the blackboard. The teacher was still busy straightening chairs.

"Can we help?" I offered.

He turned to me. "Thanks, but I'm just finishing up. By the way, I'm Mr. Williams."

"I'm Gary. This guy with his chin in his hand is Scott." Scott smiled weakly at Mr. Williams and then glared at me.

I sat down next to Scott and tried to ignore his glare. As

Mr. Williams adjusted the last few desks, the other students started drifting in. He said hello to each of them, and as he did, I really got a chance to study him.

I guess I could understand why Scott was a little upset. The guy didn't look like a science teacher at all, let alone the instructor for an Honors class. What he did look like was a basset hound. You've probably seen one. Its face is covered with wrinkles, especially on its forehead, so it always seems to be worried. Under the eyes, there are these huge bags, giving you the impression that the dog hasn't slept for days. And then the eyes! They're a deep, deep brown, and they're so sad they make you want to cry. That's what Mr. Williams looked like. He was friendly enough, but when he wasn't smiling, his face had this really sad quality about it.

Before long, the nine-o'clock bell rang. By this time there were twenty or so people sitting around the room. Scott still had his chin in his hand. Mr. Williams walked up to the front and looked out over the class.

"I think I've spoken to most of you," he said, "but in case I missed anybody, I'm Mr. Williams. This is Honors Science, and obviously it's not going to be a normal science class. One reason is that you're not normal students. I understand that you're the best science students in the entire valley." Next to me, Scott sat up a little straighter.

"The other reason is that I'm not a normal teacher. I don't like to stand up here and lecture, and I don't like textbook assignments. I like projects. I like experiments. I like field trips. You might be interested in knowing that for the past several summers I've been a forest ranger at Yosemite National Park. I'm not content just to read and talk about science. I have to *see* science in the world. Science is the study of life—of everything!" He spread his arms out wide, then slapped them down to his sides and started walking back and forth as he talked. Out of the corner of my eye, I noticed Scott leaning forward in his chair.

"We're going to do lots of projects in this class. Some of them we'll all do—for example, breeding fruit flies. Fruit flies reproduce at an incredible rate, so you'll be able to see the laws of genetics working right in front of your eyes. Other projects you'll pick yourselves. Whatever your special interest is, we'll try to accommodate you."

Scott raised his hand. "Does that include paleontology? You know, the study of fossils?"

"You bet," said Mr. Williams. "Let's see, did you say your name is Scott?" Scott nodded. "Scott, did you know there are fossils so small that you need a microscope to see them? And that when you see them magnified, their patterns are as beautiful as snowflakes?" Scott's eyes were shiny. "They're called diatoms. I'll bring some in if you'd like.

"That goes for the rest of you, too. I'll do all I can to help you round up the materials you need so that you can pursue your interests.

"One thing I'm really looking forward to with this class is field trips. There's one place we're going that I guarantee you won't forget as long as you live. It's called Lunada Bay." Mr. Williams was gesturing with every phrase. Inside of five minutes he had gone from janitor to genius.

"There'll be other field trips, too," he said, slowing his pacing down all of a sudden, "but I guess maybe I'm getting ahead of myself. Do you kids have any questions so far?"

Scott's hand shot up in the air. "When do we start?" he asked.

[8]

We
started that morning and went strong all six weeks. Mr. Williams was great. Scott and I liked him so much that pretty soon we started calling him Willy. Not to his face, of course. Just between the two of us.

Willy stuck to his word about doing lots of projects and going on trips. We were always building things or mixing things or studying things. If it wasn't amoebas, it was telescopes or flowers or sulfuric acid or octopi (that's two or more octopuses). And Willy was right about that one field trip, the one he said we'd never forget. It was a trip to Lunada Bay, which turned out to have the best tide pools on the whole West Coast. He packed us all onto a school bus at three thirty one morning so that we could be at Lunada Bay by five o'clock, when it would have the lowest tide of the year. We got there just at sunrise, and I swear the water must have been out fifty yards. All the rocks and pools that are usually underwater were exposed.

We climbed out in the middle of them and couldn't believe what we saw. We were surrounded by all the animals you always see in science books—crabs, sea urchins, starfish in three different colors, sea slugs, limpets, abalones, sand dollars, lobsters. One of the slimy ones—I can't remember which—had a funny way of defending itself. If you scared it or poked it with a stick, it would squirt its guts out at you, stomach and all. Willy told us that that didn't really hurt it, because it would just grow a new set. I was thinking that I'd like to be able to squirt my guts like that. It could come in handy. For instance, if the A9s ever tried to pants me, I could probably scare them off pretty good. Anyway, that day at Lunada Bay was fantastic. Willy really knew how to put together a field trip.

But as great as that trip was, the thing I remember best about Honors Science was *Drosophila melanogaster.* That's the scientific name for fruit flies. I'll never forget the day we started the fruit-fly project.

It was one of those really hot summer days. It must have been over a hundred degrees, and it was still only morning. The classroom wasn't air-conditioned, so you could almost see the heat rising off the desks. We were all sweating like pigs, especially Cecilia Berman, who sat next to Scott and me. Willy was in front of the class wearing one of those wrinkled shirts of his, and there were big wet rings under the arms. But in spite of the heat, he was his usual excited self.

"Okay, kids, today we start our big genetics project." He waved his arms and walked back and forth like a barker at a carnival. "We're going to breed *Drosophila melanogaster*—fruit flies. I've got normal ones, and I've got three mutant types. We'll breed them selectively and see how many of the offspring are normal and how many are mutant. Then we'll breed the offspring and see how many mutant offspring *they* have, and by the time we go through four or five generations, we should be able to see Mendel's Law at work right before our eyes."

One of the other students raised his hand. "Who's Mendel?"

"Ah, John," replied Willy, smiling broadly, "that's just the question I was hoping you'd ask. We'll talk about Mr. Mendel, but first, I wonder if I might have my good friend Al hand out one of these bottles to everyone in the class." Willy pointed to a big box full of pint milk bottles with corks in them. "All of the bottles have fruit flies and fruit-fly food in them. Our whole project will center around those bottles."

Al got up from his seat at the other end of the front row. As he walked up to the box, he looked out over the class with a wide grin. He was always doing that. Scott had labeled him a campus politician the first time he saw him. He was always grinning and patting people on the back. I think Willy was on to his game, though, because he always called him my good friend Al. Scott always called him that stupid jerk.

Al set the box on the front desk and started carrying bottles, six or seven at a time, to everybody in the room. As he did it, he walked kind of sideways so that he could grin at people and wink at them when he caught their eye. A couple of times he bumped into things because he wasn't looking where he was going.

"Gregor Mendel," Willy began, "was a nineteenth-century monk who grew pea plants in his garden. He noticed that some of the plants were tall, and some—Al, maybe you should watch where you're going—some of the plants were dwarf. He became fascinated by—hey Al, I'm serious—fascinated by the study of these plants and their variations, which today we would call dominant and recessive traits. Mendel kept notebooks—"

Willy was interrupted by a loud crash. Al had tripped over something. The bottles he was carrying had fallen on the floor and broken.

"You idiot!" Scott yelled. As Willy rushed over, you could hear a new sound in the room. Buzzing. I groaned. It was bad enough being in a hot room, but now we'd be in there with swarms of these little fruit flies.

Willy helped Al up off the floor and had him go get a broom. "It's no big thing, kids," he said, walking back to the front of the room. "These flies will be a nuisance today, but we'll just keep the windows open and most of them should be gone by tomorrow. We'll have to postpone the beginning of the project until then. Meanwhile, back to Mendel."

Calling the flies a nuisance turned out to be the understatement of the year. They were everywhere. They flew into our eyes and ears. One flew into my mouth, and I almost choked to death from coughing. I noticed that one landed on Cecilia Berman's sweaty neck and was walking around, kind of checking things out. It went down her neck and under her blouse, and it must have gotten pretty far before she felt it, because when she finally did she got this pained expression on her face and felt frantically around her chest area, if you know what I mean. She excused herself in a hurry to go to the girls' bathroom. When she got back, one side of her front was lower than the other.

When we took our break about halfway through the morning, I looked inside the sack of grapes I had brought for a snack, and I found ten or twenty fruit flies in there.

"Ugh," I said out loud. Scott looked over and saw them. He started laughing and slapping his leg.

"Now we know why they call them fruit flies," he said. "You can almost see them smacking their lips."

I decided to throw the grapes away.

The next day, the escaped fruit flies had all flown away, and we could start our project. Willy explained how to do everything, step by step. There were the normal flies, and there were three kinds of mutants: ebony, which were brown all over; vestigial-winged, which had little nubby wings instead of regular ones; and white-eyed, which had big white eyes that stared up at you when you looked at them through the magnifying glass. To breed them, you had to transfer them from bottle to bottle.

Scott loved it. "Now I know how God feels," he said. "That is, if there is a God." He was going through his agnostic stage. "Wouldn't it be a riot if there was a God, and He treated us just like we treat these fruit flies? He'd keep us all in a bottle, and then when He wanted to look at us, He'd put a chloroform cloth over the bottle and gas us. We'd all be out cold. Then He'd shake us out of the bottle and onto a paper towel."

"A paper towel?"

"Yeah, a real big one. Then He'd look at us through a magnifying glass to see who was a guy and who was a girl, and maybe He'd take a normal-type guy, like you, for instance, and dump you into another bottle with a mutant—maybe ol' Cecilia Berman."

"Hey, wait a second," I protested.

"Then He'd go away and come back later to see what the ratio of normal kids to ugly kids was."

"There wouldn't be any kids. Not with me and Cecilia Berman. No way."

Scott couldn't be stopped. "Then He'd write down the ratio in a notebook, gas you again, and put the kids in another bottle. And you know what would happen to you and ol' Cecilia, don't you?" I nodded glumly, resigned to Scott's fantasy. "To the morgue!" he said, with a look of glee on his face.

I should tell you about the morgue. It was a bottle that was half filled with formaldehyde, and so it had a terrible smell. We tried to keep it in the back of the room, where the odor wouldn't be too noticeable. The morgue was where we dumped the flies we had finished with. As soon as they had reproduced, we put them into the morgue, and they died. I guess Willy emptied the bottle every night. I sure wouldn't have wanted that job. If you want to know the truth, the morgue gave me the creeps. The thought of being dumped in there didn't do much for me, especially with that sweaty Cecilia Berman. Of course, Scott thought it was a riot. I didn't think it was so funny, because every once in a while I felt a little bad about just tossing flies into the morgue. I mean, who was I to decide whether they lived or died? Scott had made a joke about it, but we really were playing God, weren't we?

"To the morgue!" Scott kept saying. "You've outlived your usefulness, Gary. Once you've nailed ol' Cecilia, it's all over. To the morgue!"

[9]

Before we knew it, Honors Science had ended, summer was over, and school had started again. Scott and I settled back into some of our favorite routines—chess at lunch, people watching, Friday-night movies, stopping by Scott's house after school, deciding on our weekly Big Five. The only thing bad that happened was that Scott got sick a couple of times. He was absent a few days the first week of school, and then right after that he was out a week and a half. I stopped by to see him every other day or so. We played chess, and I helped him catch up on his homework. He told me he had a bad case of the flu. Except for Scott's flu, though, things went pretty well. It looked as if it would be a good year.

Even though lots of things we were doing in the eighth grade were the same as the things we did in the seventh grade, somehow it seemed different. Everything felt different. We weren't B7s anymore. We weren't even A7s.

We were B8s. To me, it was a big relief being out of the seventh grade. For one thing, I didn't have to worry about getting pantsed any longer. Scott thought it was a big relief, too, but he looked at it a little differently.

"We've paid the price, Gary," he told me as we walked home from school one day. "We've been on the bottom of the pile for a whole year. We've been called names, beaten up, spit at. . . ."

"We have?"

"Well, not literally," Scott said, "but we might as well have been. Besides, there were other things."

"Like what?"

"Like the way people laughed at us behind our backs."

"I never noticed that."

Scott gestured with one hand. "You idiot, of course you never noticed it. They did it behind our backs.

"Anyway," he went on, "now that we've paid the price, we have our chance to get back at all of them."

"How?" I asked warily.

"Like this," he said. He motioned with his head toward a group of three short, skinny guys walking a little ways ahead of us. They were B7s for sure.

"Hey, Gary," Scott said in a loud voice, "you know what's my favorite thing in the whole world?" I looked at him blankly. "Well, I'll tell you," he went on, still talking really loud and looking at the three guys ahead of us. "My favorite thing in the whole world is wasting B-Sevens."

I could see the three guys glance at each other and then pull their heads down closer to their shoulders.

"There's lots of ways you can do it," Scott said. "One way is just to sneak up behind them and smash their heads together. It's amazing how soft those little skulls are. It's just like breaking eggs.

"Another way is for two guys to grab a B-Seven, hold

him upside down by the legs, and just pull on each leg in opposite directions as hard as they can. Whoever breaks off the shortest piece gets to make a wish.

"I'll tell you one thing—this pantsing stuff is for the birds. If you're really going to waste a B-Seven, you've got to do more than just pants him. Some friends of mine caught one and didn't just take his pants off—they took everything off and made him climb up in a tree. Then they called a bunch of girls on the phone and told them to go sit under the tree if they wanted a nice surprise. After that, the kid didn't show his face at school for weeks."

The three B7s in front of us started walking faster and faster. Scott walked faster, too. I hurried to keep up with him.

"What do you think you're doing?" I whispered.

He gave me a look of grim satisfaction. "Getting back at these guys for all the time we spent in the seventh grade. We've paid our dues—now they have to pay theirs."

"What are you talking about?" I said. "These guys haven't done anything wrong. They're just three skinny B-Sevens who are scared out of their wits."

Scott kept walking fast. He wasn't looking at me. He started talking loud again.

"Another way to waste a B-Seven is to set fire to his hair. That's always interesting. Usually all you need is one guy to hold him down and one guy to light the matches. It's really pretty simple."

I couldn't take it anymore. I kept imagining myself up there with those B7s, hearing what they were hearing. I would have been about ready to faint.

So I yelled up to them, "Hey, it's okay. My friend just likes to kid around. He wouldn't hurt a flea. Besides, we were B-Sevens ourselves last year."

For the first time, the three glanced over their shoulders to see who we were. They looked at each other uncertainly, and then, not wanting to take any chances, raced off down the street.

Scott was furious. "Why did you do that?" he demanded. "I wasn't going to hurt them."

"You don't have to hit people to hurt them. They were scared to death."

"That was the whole idea—just to scare them, make them a little nervous."

"If you ask me, it was a pretty crummy thing to do," I said.

"If you ask *me*," Scott replied, "it was fine. It was just a joke."

I stared straight ahead. "I don't want to talk about it anymore."

We kept walking. I guess we went about three blocks or so without saying a word. Then we heard some footsteps behind us.

We looked back, and there, about a half block behind us, were the three B7s and two older guys, probably high-school age. These two guys were huge. They made Scott seem like a midget.

I glanced over at Scott. He looked pretty nervous.

"Let's run for it," I said. We did. But not fast enough. Actually, I was fast enough, but Scott just wasn't designed for speed. In no time at all, we were being held by these two huge guys. It was kind of uncomfortable.

"What the hell are you guys trying to do?" demanded one. He pulled one of my arms behind my back and twisted it. I winced and looked over at Scott.

"Hey, look," Scott said, "we didn't mean any harm. We were just kidding these guys. We wouldn't hurt a flea. We even told them that."

One of the B7s, a skinny kid with red hair, took a few steps toward Scott and pointed at him. "You also told us you were going to smash our heads together, and grab us by the legs and pull us apart, and take all our clothes off, and set fire to our hair!"

"Is that true?" asked one of the older guys.

Scott was starting to get desperate. "I was kidding! I swear I was kidding!"

"Really, it was just a joke," I said. "But we shouldn't have done it. I don't blame you guys for being mad. Believe me, it won't happen again."

"There's one way of making sure of it," said the other big guy. He turned to his buddy. "Okay, Jim, let's hold them. Charlie, you and your friends get one punch at each of them."

The B7s' eyes got wide. They walked up, one by one, and punched us in the stomach. The punches weren't very hard—I think the B7s were scared—but I decided it would be a good idea to act as if it really hurt. Otherwise these two big guys might want some of the action.

"Ow! Ugh!" I grunted.

Scott caught on and started doing it, too. He really hammed it up.

"Oh, my stomach! Ooh, that hurt! Boy, you guys can really punch." I gave him a dirty look.

When the B7s were finished, their friends let us go. "This'll be a warning," one of them said. "If we hear about you pulling any more of this stuff, we'll be back to take care of you personally." He turned to Scott. "And we can punch a whole lot harder than these guys." He turned and walked off, and the others followed him. Every few steps, the B7s looked back over their shoulders at us.

We waited until they were about a block away, then we picked up our books and started walking slowly home. We didn't say anything for a long time.

Finally, in a low voice, Scott said, "You didn't have to take the blame." We kept on walking, and neither of us said anything for a while longer.

Then Scott said, a little louder, "It was my fault. You didn't have to take the blame." He was looking at me now. His eyebrows were bunched together over his eyes, and his forehead was wrinkled.

I looked back at him and shrugged. "That's what friends are for," I said.

[10]

The Monday after that, Scott was absent from school again. So, as I had done before when he was absent, I got all his homework assignments from his teachers.

When I stopped by his house that afternoon, his mom answered the door and let me into the front hallway.

"Is it the flu again?" I asked her.

She had a worried look on her face. "No, apparently not. Now the doctor thinks it may be some kind of anemia."

"You mean tired blood?" I joked. "Like on the Geritol commercials?"

She laughed weakly. "Something like that, I guess."

Just then Scott came into the hallway. He was wearing a bathrobe and slippers, and he looked kind of pale. His mom smiled at him, patted his arm, and went into the other room.

"Hi, Scott," I said. "I hear you have tired blood."

"Very funny," he replied. "How was school?"

I shrugged. "Same as usual. How long do you think you'll be out this time?"

"About a week," Scott said. "That's what the doctor says, anyway. He gave me a shot and some pills and said I'd probably be able to go back to school next Monday."

"I got your homework for you again," I said. I handed him some papers with the assignments written on them.

Scott looked through them until he found the science assignment. "Hey, these questions are all about the parts of a frog," Scott said, getting suddenly excited. "Are we going to be dissecting frogs?"

"Yeah, next week," I answered.

"Fantastic!" he exclaimed. "I've always wanted to see the insides of a frog!" That sounded like the Scott I knew. I decided he couldn't be too sick if he was excited about dissecting frogs.

"I can't stay," I said. "I'm supposed to mow the lawn this afternoon. I'll come back tomorrow, and then we can talk for a while, okay?"

"Great," Scott replied. "Oh, and make sure you take good notes in science class. I don't want to make any mistakes next week when I slice up that frog."

When I went back Tuesday, Scott looked about the same. He said he felt kind of weak, so we just stayed in his room and played chess and listened to Pete Seeger albums. Scott didn't seem too worried about being sick. I think he thought of it mostly as a nuisance. He was getting bored. He had already gone through the year's back issues of *Scientific American* that his mom had checked out of the library, and I think he was even getting tired of reading *Playboy*. And since Joe Pyne was only on at night, that didn't leave Scott a whole lot to do except sleep. He told me he did a lot of sleeping, but he looked so tired that it was hard to believe.

I stopped by again on Thursday and was surprised to find that nobody was home. After knocking at the door for a long time, I finally decided that Scott's mom had probably taken him to the doctor. Except for that, I couldn't imagine any reason for him to go anyplace.

After dinner that night I called Scott's house to see what had happened. Mr. Lewis answered, which was unusual because most of the time either Scott or his mom picked up the phone.

"Hello," he said.

"Hi, Mr. Lewis. It's Gary."

"Oh, hi, Gary. How are you?" That was odd. First of all, Mr. Lewis never said, "How are you?" He always said, "Who are you going to vote for?" At least, he always said that to me. It was kind of a running joke between us. He knew I didn't care that much for politics. The other odd thing was his voice. It was shaky. Usually it was either really excited and loud, or else kind of soft and far away and dreamy, like when he was talking about world peace and brotherhood. But this was the first time I had heard that it was shaky.

"I'm fine," I answered, not knowing what else to say. "I'm just calling to see how Scott's doing."

"Now, I don't want this to upset you, Gary," he said, "but Scott's in the hospital. The doctor wanted to run some tests on him for a few days. It's strictly routine, so I don't want you to get upset."

I hadn't noticed it before, but I could hear myself breathing into the phone. It was almost as if I had been running and were out of breath.

"What kind of tests?" I asked, trying to take slow and steady breaths.

"Oh, the usual sort of thing. Urine tests, blood tests, all the normal tests."

"But why did they have to put him in the hospital?"

"The doctor felt it would be more convenient that way. Really, it's nothing to worry about." His voice was still shaking a little bit. "As a matter of fact, I was just on my way to see him when you called. His mother's already over there."

"Could I come?" I asked.

"Uh—no, not this time. Try calling Mrs. Lewis tomorrow. Maybe you could work something out with her. Anyway," he added quickly, "I've got to get going."

"Okay, I'll call tomorrow."

"Do that. And don't worry. I'm sure this is nothing serious. Talk to you later, Gary." He hung up.

"Good-bye," I said into the phone. I just stood there holding it.

My mother stuck her head through the doorway. "Let me know when you're off the phone."

"I'm done," I answered, putting the phone back on the hook.

She came into the room. "Who was that you were talking to?" she asked me absentmindedly.

"Mr. Lewis. He says they took Scott to the hospital for a few days to run some tests on him."

She got this almost frightened look on her face. I suddenly had the feeling she wished she hadn't asked the question. Sometimes I think Mom believes that if you're careful to ask the right questions and say the right things, you'll never find out about anything sad or painful. She hates sad, painful things.

I couldn't stand to see her looking like that. "Mr. Lewis told me it's nothing serious. Just some routine tests."

She looked relieved. Maybe I was still worried, but at

least Mom wasn't scared anymore. I hated to have her scared. That was one problem I didn't need.

[11]

When
I called Mrs. Lewis on Friday, she said I should wait until
Saturday to go see Scott. She told me technically I wasn't
allowed to visit him, since I was under fourteen. But she
had found out that people do it all the time, and that if my
mom went along, I probably wouldn't have any trouble. I
thought it was pretty nice of her to check into it for me.
To tell you the truth, though, I wished I could have gone
by myself. I was feeling nervous enough without Mom
bursting into tears or telling Scott she'd pray for him.

Visiting hours started at eleven in the morning, so on
Saturday Mom and I went over to the hospital at eleven
o'clock sharp. On TV, hospitals look like pretty normal
places. You get used to seeing all your favorite stars
walking in the halls or lying sick in bed. But now that I've
actually been in a hospital, I can tell you that in real life,
hospitals aren't like that at all. They give me the creeps.
Nurses and attendants are always wheeling people down

the hallway on tables, and I wonder where they're taking them. The doctors are always being paged on the PA, and I imagine someone up in a back room someplace, dying, waiting for the doctor to arrive. I always have the feeling something terrible is happening just around the corner.

The first thing I remember noticing about the hospital that Saturday morning was that there were no colors except white and a kind of dull green. The floors, the walls, the curtains, even the doctors and nurses—white or green. And besides looking strange, the place smelled strange, like a doctor's office. You could smell the shots and the Band-Aids and the iodine and the alcohol, and on top of that there seemed to be a smell kind of like floor wax. I think I would almost rather have smelled the B.O. in the locker room at school. At least you knew it was from people.

I remember looking down those long hospital hallways. It reminded me of places where you have two mirrors facing each other. What you get looking into those mirrors is reflections of reflections of reflections, until it looks as if the room went on forever, repeating itself over and over again. That's what those halls were like. You could hardly see the end of them, they were so long. And every door and light and fire extinguisher on the wall was repeated again and again. Even the doctors and nurses who walked up and down the halls seemed to look alike.

Maybe it was because the hallways all looked the same, or maybe it was just because it was our first time there, but whatever it was, somehow Mom and I got lost. I guess we made a wrong turn somewhere. I noticed that the numbers were getting smaller, not bigger. Then, when we went back in the direction of the bigger numbers, they stopped all of a sudden and jumped back to zero.

"I thought you said you had it all figured out," Mom said. "You told me you knew exactly where you were going."

"His room's got to be right around here someplace," I mumbled, trying to ignore her. "Let's see, this hallway over here looks familiar. Maybe this is where we made our wrong turn."

It wasn't. We went up and down the hallways, with me in front and Mom following. I glanced in some of the rooms as we went past. There were old people in some, lying in bed, staring at the ceiling. In other rooms, there were regular people visiting the patients. They all whispered or spoke in low voices, as if they didn't want to upset anyone. In a few of the rooms, the patients were lying on their side, looking through the open door to see what was going on in the hallway. As soon as they looked at me, I would turn my head away so they wouldn't think I had some kind of morbid curiosity. Sometimes a low moan would come from one of the rooms. I couldn't decide whether I should stop one of the doctors in the hall and tell him about it. I ended up just hurrying on by and trying not to hear it.

In every corridor there was a waiting room. When we passed one of those, I'd look inside, and I'd always see the same thing. There would be people sitting in chairs, all facing toward a TV set in the corner. Nobody would be talking. They'd just be staring at the TV, watching whatever happened to be on. In this case, it was Saturday morning, so they were all watching cartoon shows. It was pretty ridiculous. Here were these people, probably waiting to hear whether their relatives were going to live or die, and they were staring at Bugs Bunny or the Flintstones.

Every once in a while, I'd look back over my shoulder

to see if Mom was still there. One time when I did that, something terrible happened. I ran into a bed that a nurse was wheeling down the hall with a patient on it. I guess I jolted the guy pretty good, because I heard him groan. I looked down at him and saw that his face was almost the same color as the sheets that were covering him. His lips were dry and chapped, and they were moving a little bit as if he were trying to say something.

"Hey, I'm really sorry," I said quickly. "Honest, I mean it. I'm sorry." I looked up at the nurse. "I'm sorry."

She gave me a cold stare. "Just watch where you're going, young man."

I felt awful. That guy was sick. I might have killed him, bumping up against him like that. If he could have talked, he probably would have sworn at me and called me all sorts of names. I would have deserved them, too. I looked back at Mom.

"I didn't mean to, Mom," I said. She patted my shoulder.

We kept walking through the halls, but now I went a little slower. Just when I was about to decide that we'd never find Scott, we saw what looked like the right number above one of the doors.

"I think this is it, Mom," I said. She checked the piece of paper in her purse to make sure, and then she looked up at me and nodded. I glanced up at the room number one last time. Scott was just a few feet away. Maybe he was lying in bed staring at the ceiling, like those other patients. Maybe his lips were cracked and he would have trouble talking, like the man I ran into. There was no way of telling. I swallowed hard and walked through the door.

[12]

It wasn't a big room, but squeezed inside were three beds and three people. In the bed nearest the door, there was an old man who seemed to be sleeping. On the far side of the room was another bed, and in it, sitting up, was a middle-aged man wearing glasses and reading a book. Straight ahead of us was a third bed, with Scott in it. He was reading, too—*Scientific American,* naturally.

My first impression of him was that he seemed awfully pale. Even the freckles on his nose had faded. My second impression was that, except for being pale, he really looked pretty normal. Maybe a little weaker than usual, but basically normal.

"Hi, Scott," I said quietly, not wanting to disturb anybody.

Scott looked up. "Hey, Gary. How's it going?" he said in his normal loud voice. "Oh, and hi, Mrs. Matthews." He motioned to two nearby chairs.

"Hello, Scott," Mom replied, as we sat down. "I understand it's nothing serious."

I shot her a quick look, and she blinked real fast a couple of times.

Her comment didn't seem to bother Scott, though. "That's what the tests showed," he remarked. "The doctor thought maybe I had mono or something—"

I must have had a puzzled expression on my face, because he paused and explained, "Mono is short for mononucleosis. It's a blood disease that makes you real weak and keeps you sick for months sometimes.

"Anyway, my mom and dad said the tests came out negative. They talked to the doctor last night. I guess I just have anemia. The doctor's giving me some treatments for it."

Mom's face relaxed. "Your parents were right, then. It *is* nothing serious. We can thank God for that." I squirmed. Mom sat back in her chair, having gotten the information she wanted.

"So how did all this happen?" I asked. "One day you were at home, and the next day you were in the hospital."

"Well," he began, "I guess it was Thursday morning when I woke up and felt really terrible. I was so weak I just wanted to lie in bed the rest of my life. Plus I ached all over—like when you get the flu, only much worse. My mom called the doctor, and he made a special trip to see me. He checked me over and asked me to tell him exactly how I felt, and when I did, he told my mom he wanted to put me in the hospital for a few days and run some tests. So they brought me in here and started poking me with needles and taking X rays and looking into my eyes. They took some blood, too. Do you want to see my arm?" Before I could answer, he stuck out his left arm, and in the crook of it was a dark-red bruise.

"Ugh," I said. "That looks awful. Hey, why did it bruise like that? They took some of my blood once, and it didn't make a bruise."

He shrugged his shoulders. "I don't know. Maybe it's my anemia. Anyway, with the tests and the way I was already feeling, I was pretty bad off all day Thursday. But I managed to get some sleep that night, and Friday morning I felt a lot better. That was yesterday. I was still really tired, though, so I slept most of the day. My mom was here just about all day, and then my dad came over right after work, and they talked to the doctor. That's when they told me I didn't have mono. So the doctor says I can probably go home Monday. But I won't be able to go back to school for another week or so."

"Well," I said, "at least now they know what's wrong with you. I'm sure glad you don't have mono."

"Yeah, but this means I'll miss science class next week. I won't be able to dissect a frog. I was really looking forward to that."

About that time, Scott reached down for something under the bed. As he leaned over, the sheet fell away, and I could see that his hospital gown had no back to it. His butt was sticking right up in the air.

"I like your dress," I said.

He sat up straight all of a sudden and tugged at the gown. For a minute he wasn't pale.

"This stupid thing. They won't let you wear your own pajamas around here. When you check in, they give you this dumb outfit with no back on it. Every time you get out of bed you have to hold the back of it together so people can't see anything. It's embarrassing."

I tried to picture big, rugged Scott mincing across the linoleum floor with this little wispy hospital gown, holding it together like a girl with a wide skirt on a windy day.

I couldn't help giggling, and I noticed that Mom was giggling a little bit, too.

Scott glared at me. Then, careful to keep the sheet pulled around him, he reached over again and lifted something out from under the bed. It was his portable chess set.

"How about a quick game?"

We played three games of chess, and he won all three.

Scott came home from the hospital Monday morning, so that afternoon I stopped by to see him. He surprised me by answering the door himself, wearing a T-shirt, jeans, and sneakers. Except for being a little pale still, he didn't even look sick.

"Hi, Gary," he said. "Come on in. I want to show you something." He led me back to his room. As we passed the living room, I saw Mrs. Lewis and said hello to her. She was looking through an old photo album.

When we got to his room, Scott explained, "Today I got tired of reading, so just for fun I pulled out the phone book and decided to look up the very last name. It was Wasyl Zyzz. Can you believe that?" he asked, with a big smirk on his face. "So I got this idea of looking through the phone book for other funny names.

"Look at this," he said. He motioned toward the bed, where I saw a pad of paper, a pencil, and an open telephone book. He handed me the pad. It was a list of names, printed in Scott's awkward style, with smudges and fingerprints all over it.

Scott pointed to the top name. "Wilberforce Gackle," he said. "That's somebody's name, right out of that phone book. Wilberforce Gackle. Can you imagine somebody giving their son a name like that? It's bad enough having a name like Gackle without people calling you Wilberforce." He screwed up his face, hunched over, and wriggled his finger at me. "Wilberforce, empty the trash. Wilberforce, help me across the street. Wilberforce, straighten your bow tie." Scott started to laugh. I was having more and more trouble picturing him sick.

"Look at the next one—Hannibal Fiebelkorn!" he roared, slapping his leg. "And what's the one after that?"

"Stoats van Oostendorp, Junior," I read.

Scott was beside himself. "Oost—Oost—" he gasped.

I was starting to get into the spirit of it. "Emerald Quackenbush," I read, giggling. "Noah Basket, M.D. Zoltan Purifoy. T. Hee Quigley." By this time I was giggling uncontrollably. In between giggles, I managed to whoop, "Balthazar P. Dern. Lafady Lafady. Dimple Teeter."

Scott looked over my shoulder at the list. "I wonder what these people look like," he said, still laughing.

"I bet Lyman Nase is a wimp," I giggled. "F. R. Shucks is probably an old guy who wears wrinkled clothes and never washes under his arms."

Scott broke in. "Ida Izitz is an old-maid librarian with glasses and a pointed nose. Rupert Rideout—he's got to be a matinee idol. Oswald Gasser runs a service station."

"Bartell Cleave is a butcher," I added. "Ernie Friedgut is a short-order cook. Philander Q. Icenbice, Junior, is an exterminator."

Scott started slapping his leg again. "Philander Q. Icenbice, Junior," he roared.

"I bet Lowell Limpopo works at McDonald's," I went on. "Agatha Creech has a shrill voice and is always yelling at people. Norbert Bube—"

Scott was helpless with laughter, bent over double, holding his stomach. There was no sound coming out of his mouth. His face was bright red, and his mouth was open so wide he almost looked in pain.

Just then, his mom walked by the open door and saw Scott. "Oh, my God!" she shrieked, and rushed into the room. She cradled his head in her arms and led him to the bed. She put his head in her lap and started stroking his hair.

"Scott," she said, "does it hurt bad?"

Scott looked up at her. His face was still red, and his eyes were wet and puffy from laughing.

"Mom, what are you talking about?" he asked. "I'm fine. We were just laughing really hard."

Her shoulders slumped down, and she hugged him to her.

"Thank God," she said softly.

[13]

"The world belongs to extroverts, kids. No one's going to come up to you, shake your hand, and say, 'You must be John Smith—I've heard you're a terrific person.' The world's just not like that."

It had been a month since the funny-names list. Scott had returned to school three weeks ago, and everything was back to normal. Everything, that is, except Mrs. McNeill, our English teacher. She was never normal. She was always springing surprises on the class, and I was sure that today would be no exception.

"Most of the time the world's just not a very friendly place," Mrs. McNeill went on. "No one's going to notice you unless you *make* them notice. It's *your* responsibility, not theirs." She was charging around the room, waving her arms in the air. Every once in a while she'd stop to catch a student's eye for emphasis. She was one of those people you either love or hate. Lots of people didn't like her unpredictable style. As for me, I just figured she was a little eccentric. I enjoyed it. I learned a lot in her class and was entertained at the same time. Scott wasn't too crazy about her, though. Except for answering her questions, I doubt that he had spoken to her once all semester.

"The reason I'm making such an issue of this," she went on, "is that I marked your five-week progress reports last night, and I discovered I have no earthly idea who some of those names in my roll book are. We've spent five weeks together in this class, and some of you kids are still perfect strangers to me. It's incredible!"

She walked to her desk and picked up the roll book. "Now, for example, Arthur Aronsen—who is this person?" A little dark-haired kid in the back of the room raised his hand. "Arthur, would you please go and stand in front of the class?

"Janice Bradley—let's see, you're the girl who wants to be an astronomer. Stephanie Compinski—you have those awful shoes with taps that drive me crazy. Brian Feldman—you're the eighth-grade president. Shana Fenstermacher—hmm. Sorry, Shana, but I don't know who you are. You can join Mr. Aronsen at the front of the class." A big fat girl waddled up the aisle and stood next to Arthur Aronsen. Somebody snickered. Mrs. McNeill whirled around and spotted a blond kid who had his hand over his mouth.

"And who, sir, are you?" she demanded.

"Roy Wallace," he answered.

"You could have fooled me," snapped Mrs. McNeill. "Up to the front with you, too." His smile sagged, and he shuffled up to where the others were.

I was starting to get nervous. I wasn't worried about whether Mrs. McNeill would know me, because I was always answering questions and volunteering for things, but I was worried about Scott. He hadn't even been there for most of the semester. And even if he had, English wasn't exactly his favorite subject. He thought it was a big waste of time to read novels about things that never really happened, and he thought it was even a bigger waste of time to sit around talking about them. So he never said much in class. He would just kind of sit there, looking uncomfortable. The fact that he was tall should have made him stand out in class, but he always slumped down in his chair, kind of like his dad, so he didn't seem to be that big. All in all, I was willing to bet that Mrs. McNeill hadn't noticed him.

She continued down the list of names in her roll book. "Martha Jencks—let's see, you're the pianist. Barry Kent—Mr. Kent, I know exactly who you are because you, of course, are five minutes late to class every day. And though it may seem unfair to some of your prompt, anonymous classmates, I won't make you go to the front of the class. The fact is, you've made a name for yourself, even though it's a bad name." She glanced down at her roll book. Scott was next.

"Scott Lewis." She looked up at Scott. I cringed. "Scott Lewis—" All of a sudden, her eyes had a soft, deep look. "Yes, of course, Scott."

Before I could figure out what she meant by that, she was reading my name. "Gary Matthews—Gary, you could be a very good writer if you didn't insist on starting every essay, 'Since the beginning of time . . .' I'm tired of reading about 'the sweep of history' and 'man's finest achievements'! What's wrong with right now? And what's wrong with little things, like coffee cups and apple cores and spools of thread? Aren't they important enough? You and every other thirteen-year-old boy in the world seem to feel the need to solve the world's problems each time you sit down to write. It's boy prose—pompous, puffed up, and perfectly absurd!" I felt everybody in the whole class staring at me. I looked down and started cleaning my fingernails.

After she had gone all the way through Harry Zimmerman, she put the roll book down on her desk, crossed her arms in front of her, and stared at the seven people standing in front of her. They looked scared to death. A couple of them looked as if they were going to be sick.

"Welcome to life," Mrs. McNeill said. "Maybe at home your mothers and fathers take you by the hand and wait patiently for you to speak up. Maybe you can depend on your friends to show some interest in you. But in the real world, things just don't happen that way. People are too busy to stop and wait for you to crawl out of your shell. Unless you step forward and let people know who you are, you'll get lost in the shuffle. You'll be last in every line, and all the extroverts and loudmouths will be in front of you when the goodies are handed out."

While she was talking, I kept hearing fidgeting sounds coming from the desk next to me. I glanced over there. It was Brian Feldman, the eighth-grade president. Brian was always bragging about how he was going to be a famous civil-rights lawyer when he grew up. As Mrs. McNeill talked, he kept shifting in his seat. His eyes were narrow, and he had wrinkles all across his forehead. His neck and ears were redder than usual, and he was shaking his head slowly from side to side.

"You've had five weeks in this class to let me know who you are," Mrs. McNeill went on. "Maybe you're a sharp dresser. Or a comedian. Maybe you're always late, like Mr. Kent. Maybe you write boy prose, like our friend Mr. Matthews." I could feel my cheeks get hot. "Somehow, some way, you should have made yourself known to me."

Brian Feldman couldn't take it anymore. "Mrs. McNeill," he exploded, "I think you're being cruel to these people. What right do you have to embarrass them in front of everybody like this?" There were murmurs of agreement. Brian's face was getting redder by the minute. "It's easy for you to stand up there and call out names and pass judgment on everybody, but how do you think they feel? They have rights, too, you know. It's not fair— it's just not fair."

Everyone turned to Mrs. McNeill to see what she'd say. She smoothed her dress and folded her hands and just stared down at the floor for a minute. Then she did a funny thing. Instead of looking up at Brian, she looked at Scott, as if he'd been the one who had challenged her. Her eyes had the same deep look they'd had when she had called his name a few minutes before. Her voice was low, and there was something about it that all of a sudden made me feel like crying.

"You're right," she said to Scott. "It isn't at all fair. But it's life, and whoever said that life was fair?" The bell rang, but she just kept gazing at Scott. When we left the room, she was still standing there with her hands folded, staring at Scott's empty desk.

[14]

The next day, Scott was absent. It worried me, because I thought maybe he had come down with anemia again.

In English, Mrs. NcNeill asked me to see her after class. When the bell rang, I went up to her desk.

"Gary," she said, "I'd like to talk to you for a minute about your last composition." She motioned for me to come around the desk and sit next to her. Then she opened the briefcase that sat next to her chair and took out my composition, but just then, Mr. Merrick stuck his head in the door.

"Could I see you for just one second, Mrs. McNeill?"

She nodded and turned to me. "I'll be right back, Gary."

When she'd gone, I glanced idly into her briefcase, which she'd left standing there on the floor. You know how it is when you're not looking at anything in particular. Sometimes words jump out at you from the middle of a page. The words were *Scott Lewis*. They were part of a hand-written letter.

Before I had time to think about it, I was reading the rest of the letter:

Dear Mrs. McNeill,

Our son, Scott Lewis, has been absent recently from your class. We thought you should know why.

Scott has leukemia. As you know, this is a fatal disease. The doctor tells us that he may live for a short time or a long time. There is no way of telling for sure.

Scott will be coming to school as much as he can. Sometimes he might look very sick, and this is why we thought you and his other teachers should know the situation. We are not telling anyone else, including Scott. He is too young to know, and other people might not understand. Please don't tell anyone.

We would appreciate it if you would do what you can to make Scott happy and comfortable while he is in your class.

Sincerely,
Norman Lewis

I sat there staring at the letter. Just then, I heard Mrs. McNeill coming back. I quickly looked around the room—at the blackboard, at the ceiling, at the floor, anyplace but the briefcase. I couldn't let her know that I had seen the letter.

"Now," she said, "where were we?" She sat back down at the desk. "Oh, yes, your composition . . ."

As she went on, I tried to listen, but I couldn't understand what she was saying. Her words seemed blurred.

Scott was going to die. I thought about that as I watched Mrs. McNeill talk and gesture. Just then I noticed a spider walking across the desk in front of me. It wasn't a big spider. It was just a little brown spider, moving across the desk toward where my hands were clenched together. It walked up one side of my hands, across the knuckles. I could feel it gliding along. It went over the top of my thumbs and down the other side, going in and out between my fingers. It would disappear and reappear as it made its way down. Then the spider was back on the table, scuttling across the wood and underneath some papers. Scott was going to die. I just sat there and turned it over in my mind. I wasn't sad. I wasn't angry. I wasn't scared. I just sat there.

I became aware of Mrs. McNeill's voice. ". . . so do you have any questions, Gary?"

"No, ma'am," I mumbled.

She looked at me. "Are you all right? You look a little pale."

"I'm okay," I said. "I guess maybe I should get going to my next class."

"I suppose you should," she said, and wrote me out a tardy excuse. As she handed it to me, she studied my face.

"Are you sure you're all right?" she asked.

I nodded and got up from the chair. A moment later I was out of the classroom and walking down the deserted hallway.

If this had been a movie, I would have held back my tears until I got into the hall, and then, once I was by myself, I would have leaned against the row of lockers and started sobbing. But that's not what happened at all. When I left Mrs. McNeill's office, I just walked down the hall as I would have done any other time. I noticed the candy wrappers on the floor and the words scribbled on the wall and the broken clock that had shown 5:26 all semester. I walked past old Mr. Travis's government class, and he was droning on, the same as usual. I went to my locker, and inside was the same ratty science book that I'd brought to school that morning. Everything was normal. No tears, no nothing.

I walked into science class and gave Mr. Balakian my tardy excuse. I sat down and opened my notebook to start taking notes. The way Mr. Balakian had the desks set up, the class was split into two parts, with one half facing the other and an aisle down the middle where he lectured. As I listened to him lecture, I noticed that Sherry Fein, who sat across from me in the first row, was wearing a short skirt that was up around her thighs. I could look right up her skirt and see her panties. They were light blue. I casually slumped down in my seat so I could get a better view. At first I just glanced over at her for a second at a time, but then the glances got longer and longer. I couldn't keep my eyes off those light-blue panties. And then Sherry Fein must have looked over and seen me staring, because she snapped her legs together, tugged at her skirt, and shot me a really dirty look. And all of a sudden I felt just terrible.

What kind of person looks up a girl's skirt while his best friend is dying? Scott was probably in bed right now, maybe in pain, and here I was trying to get a clear shot of Sherry Fein's light-blue panties. What was wrong with me? Why didn't I feel anything? Why hadn't I gotten upset when I found out this terrible thing about Scott? Any normal person would have shouted or screamed or cried. I had just sat there.

I told myself that I didn't show my emotions much. Maybe that wasn't the truth. Maybe the truth was that I didn't have any emotions to show. Maybe the truth was that I was some kind of freak.

[15]

When school was over that day, I didn't feel like going straight home. And I sure didn't feel like stopping by to see Scott. I didn't know how I'd ever face him again. Besides, if he was really sick, he probably didn't feel like talking to anyone.

So I decided to walk over to a park not far from school. It was a good place to wander around and just think. There were plenty of trees, a baseball diamond, a few benches to sit on, and a lake. There weren't many people there that day, probably because it was cold and windy. I had on my heavy coat, though, and so I stuffed my hands in my pockets and just started walking. I didn't have anything to carry, because I had left all my books at school. I couldn't see myself studying that night.

There were a couple of little kids fishing in the lake. They were crouched by the edge of the water, with their coats pulled up over their ears, shivering. They had these miniature poles that they sell at the dime store. The kids reminded me of Scott. He liked to go fishing every once in a while. Last summer he had gotten a pole and tackle box for his birthday. On weekends sometimes, he and his dad would drive out to a lake and fish all day. I went with them a few times. Not that I fished. I just went along to watch. It got pretty funny sometimes. Scott's dad would set up his folding chair at the edge of the lake, cast out, lean back, and slide into his talking position. Then he'd start in about equal opportunity and the advantages of socialism. Scott wouldn't hear a thing. While his dad babbled on, he'd bait his hook and cast out, and then he'd start muttering to the fish, as if he were angry at them. It was as if he were at war with them. He'd call them names and insult them, and if they hadn't bitten in ten or fifteen seconds, he'd reel in as fast as he could, check his bait, and then cast out into enemy territory again. All this time his dad would just be sitting there, talking away as though Scott were listening.

I walked past the kids at the lake and wandered over toward the trees. Underneath the trees there was a layer of dead leaves that crunched when you walked through them. I heard soft voices coming from up ahead, and I noticed a dark shape on the ground. It was a blanket, and rolled up in it were a boy and a girl with their arms around each other. They must have been high-school age. Their noses were practically touching, and they were talking and gazing into each other's eyes. They were so wrapped up in each other that they didn't realize I was there, even though I'd been crunching through the leaves.

I just stood there and watched. They seemed to be having a great time. I wondered what it was like, being so close to somebody like that. I guess having a girl friend is an experience that everybody has sooner or later. Everybody but Scott. Scott would never have a girl friend. He'd never lie under trees in a park, wrapped in a blanket with somebody he really liked. Maybe he would never even kiss anybody. I mean, except for his mom and his grandparents and people like that. It seems that everybody should have the chance to kiss somebody, eventually anyway. I'm not sentimental or anything, but kissing just seems like something everybody should do at least once.

I guess I could say the same for sex. Not that I know much about it. I couldn't imagine what it would be like to take your clothes off and be naked with a girl, let alone do the things they talk about in biology class. And I especially couldn't imagine Scott doing it. He just didn't look like the type. He wasn't too coordinated, for one thing. He'd probably bump his head or something. But it made me mad to think he'd never even have the chance to try it. I knew he was interested. He enjoyed those *Playboy* magazines as much as anybody. What gave me the right to have sex someday when Scott would never be able to? Why did I get to grow up when Scott may never be more than thirteen years old? Why did I deserve to live when Scott was going to die?

I turned around and walked out from under the trees. I didn't care if the couple heard me leave. I walked back past the two little kids who were still shivering by the lake. I felt like going home.

Ten minutes later I was closing the front door behind me.

"Gary, is that you?" came Mom's voice from the kitchen.

"Yeah," I said, pulling off my coat.

"How was school?"

"Okay."

She came out of the kitchen and faced me across the living room. "You're a little late. Did you and Scott stop by his house?"

"Scott is—sick today."

"Maybe you should call him to see how he's doing."

"I'll call him when I feel like calling him," I snapped. "It's not my fault if he's sick." I turned, stomped back to my room, and slammed the door. I threw my coat at the chair and flopped down onto the bed.

I thought about the letter again. It had said not to tell anyone about Scott. But even if I had permission to tell, whom could I have told? I couldn't say anything to Mom, because she'd probably get hysterical. I couldn't talk to Dad, period. I couldn't tell anyone at school, because I didn't really have any other friends. And I couldn't tell Mrs. McNeill, because she'd think I'd been snooping in her briefcase. The one person I could have gone to was Scott. And he wasn't allowed to know what was happening to his own body.

Leukemia. Scott had leukemia. I stared straight ahead with my chin resting on my hands. The letter had said leukemia was a fatal disease, but that didn't tell me much. All of a sudden I wanted to know more about it.

I rolled off the bed and went over to the bookcase. I pulled out the "L" volume of the encyclopedia and sat on the edge of the bed. I leafed through it until I found the right page.

"LEUKEMIA, *loo KEE mee uh,*" I read to myself, "is a serious disease of the white cells of the blood. The disease is a purposeless, continual growth of white blood cells. The uncontrolled growth of these cells harms the body in many ways. Useless white cells flood the tissues and blood. The bone marrow loses its ability to produce red blood cells, and blood production is affected. This leads to anemia." I looked up for a second. So Scott did have anemia after all. The only problem was, that wasn't all he had. "People with leukemia may have an enlarged spleen and enlarged lymph glands. They may also bleed easily." I shivered. Somehow, having too many white blood cells didn't give me the creeps the way bleeding did.

I read on:

> The disease attacks both children and adults. There is no known cure for leukemia, although some cases may go on for many years. Doctors can temporarily relieve the symptoms of the disease through the use of blood transfusions and doses of cortisone and chemicals called antimetabolites. But the abnormal growth of the white blood cells returns, and eventually causes the death of the patient.
>
> Leukemia can be either acute or chronic. Acute leukemia progresses rapidly, and the patient may die within a few months. Chronic leukemia develops more slowly and may continue for five to twenty-five years.

So no one knew how long Scott was going to live. He might be alive for six more weeks or six more years. All they knew was that leukemia was eventually going to kill him. Scott was going to die.

I closed the encyclopedia and put it back on the shelf. I lay back on the bed and stared up at the ceiling. Usually when I did that, it was because I wanted to think. Today I just wanted to lie there.

Pictures kept flashing through my mind. It was as if somebody were projecting slides in my head and I didn't have any control over them. There were the two kids fishing in the lake. Scott was dropping fruit flies into the morgue, laughing. Mom and I were walking through the hallway in the hospital. Scott and I were playing chess on the lunch benches at school. The couple in the park were bundled up against each other, talking softly and smiling. Scott was bent over double laughing, with his face all red, and his mother came rushing over to him.

One picture kept flashing back, over and over again. It was Scott, lying dead in his coffin with his hands folded across his chest. What gave me the creeps were his eyes. They weren't closed. They were open, staring straight ahead. That picture kept coming back. I couldn't stop it. There was Scott, right in front of me, dead. And then I realized it wasn't Scott at all I was seeing. It was me, lying there with my hands folded across my chest, staring straight ahead—just like I was doing now.

I must have yelled, because Mom came bursting through the door, looking scared to death.

"What happened?"

I looked up at her, but I was still seeing that picture of me in the coffin. I shivered.

Mom came over closer to the edge of the bed. She looked really frightened. "Gary, what is it?"

I didn't want her to know anything was wrong. "Don't worry, Mom," I managed. "I was just having a bad dream. I feel better now."

She wrinkled her forehead and looked at me for a few seconds. Then she nodded weakly and drifted out of the room, glancing back once to make sure I was still all right.

[16]

I had
trouble putting that awful picture out of my mind. Sometimes Scott was in the coffin; sometimes I was. Whoever
it was, the eyes would always be open wide, staring.
The picture kept following me around. The more I tried
to forget it, the stronger it got.

The next morning when Dad drove me to school, it was
on the windshield of the car. In first period, it was on the
blackboard. In second period, when I was taking a test, it
was on my answer sheet. I kept forgetting the answers I
was going to write down. When I went to my locker
before third period to get my English books, there it was
on the inside of the door. I just stood there looking at it,
getting goose bumps.

"Aren't you even going to welcome me back?" asked a
familiar voice from behind me. I spun around, and there
was Scott.

"Hey, you don't look too good," he said. "Your face is

all white. I thought I was supposed to be the one who's been sick." I just stood there. I was having trouble orienting myself. "Are you okay?" he asked in a different voice.

I nodded my head. "Yeah, I guess so," I mumbled. "Yeah, I'm fine, really," I said, trying to sound normal.

That seemed to satisfy him, because all of a sudden he got this irritated expression on his face and demanded, "What happened yesterday? I kept waiting for you to stop by or call, but you never did."

I fumbled around for an answer. "I didn't . . . know how sick you were. I didn't want to disturb you or anything."

"Disturb me? I was bored stiff. I didn't want to stay home in the first place, but Mom heard me sniffling a little bit when I got up and told me she thought I'd better stay home from school. It was ridiculous. I don't know what she was so worried about."

I was finally alert enough to get a good look at him. He appeared to be as healthy as I was.

"I *wanted* you to disturb me," Scott went on. "I thought maybe we could listen to Pete Seeger and play chess."

"Scott, I'm sorry," I said. "Look, it won't happen again." I felt terrible. I shut my locker, and we moved off in the direction of English class.

English was tough for me that day. When Mrs. McNeill saw Scott, she seemed as surprised as I had been, and I was suddenly reminded that I wasn't the only one who knew about the leukemia. It was as if there were two different classes going on at the same time. In one, the subject was adverbs and adjectives, and people were writing on the blackboard and asking questions. In the other, the subject was Scott. Mrs. McNeill and Scott and I were the only ones in that class. It was as if the room were empty except for the three of us.

The whole thing reminded me of dinner at my house when Mom and Dad were arguing. We would sit there eating, with this argument on our minds. They'd be mad at each other, thinking of how mean or stupid or unfair the other one was. I'd be trying to figure out a way to make them stop being angry. But all three of us would act as if nothing were wrong. We'd pretend everything was fine. Mom would ask Dad how work had been. Dad would tell us about something that had happened at the office. I would go over my day at school. Sometimes the difference between what was going on inside of me and outside of me got really confusing, and I'd get a headache. That's what was happening that day in English class. My head was throbbing.

When the bell rang, I rushed out of the room and waited for Scott in the hallway. He gave me a funny look when he came out, but I just ignored it. I was afraid that if we started talking about how I was feeling, Scott would get the idea I was covering something up, and then it would just be that much harder to keep the secret. And I had to keep that secret. I couldn't let him down. I wasn't going to be the one to tell Scott he was dying.

I remember in Honors Science how Willy once told us that understanding something—whether it's genetics or a casserole recipe or just life in general—is a matter of fitting things together. You fit the little details in with the big picture; you fit what you don't know in with what you do know; you fit what you think in with what you see and hear. If you keep working at it, things will start making sense.

I wanted to understand what was happening to Scott, but I just couldn't fit things together. The letter had said that Scott was dying, but it didn't fit in with anything else. He looked perfectly normal. He and I played chess at noon, listened to folk-music records, chose the Big Five every week, and went to movies on Friday nights, the same as always. He never complained about feeling bad. He wasn't acting like dying people are supposed to act.

The day I had found out about Scott, he was absent from school, and that fit. It made sense that someone who was dying would be absent from school. But when he came back to school the next day looking fine, I started getting confused, and I was getting more confused every day.

So what I started doing was just not thinking about it. I'd act as if nothing had changed. Sometimes it actually worked. I'd go for as many as two or three hours without thinking about Scott dying. But then it would pop back into my head without any warning, and in the strangest places. In the bathroom, for instance, or while running laps in gym class, or mowing the lawn. Sometimes the whole idea seemed so crazy that I'd wonder whether the letter had been a dream.

When I was with Scott, I tried my hardest just to relax and enjoy myself. Most of the time it didn't work too well, but once in a while I'd get in the spirit of it, especially when we were laughing about something. That's when the whole business about Scott dying seemed the craziest. At times like that, it was all I could do to keep from just casually mentioning, "Hey, I heard the dumbest thing the other day. I heard that you're dying. Isn't that crazy?"

Sometimes when we were together, I felt like I couldn't hold it inside anymore or I'd explode. It seemed to happen a lot when we were playing chess. I couldn't stand the silence in between moves. I'd start talking to him in my head, saying things like, "Scott, you don't know it, but you're dying. You may feel fine now, but pretty soon you'll be back in the hospital." The longer the silence was, the louder my voice inside would get. Before long it would be shouting so loud I'd think he would hear it for sure. "Scott! You're dying! Don't just sit there! Can't you hear me? You're dying!" Once, it got so bad I had to get up and go into the other room. I was sure that any minute I was going to start shouting it out loud.

At home, I was tempted to try to work it into the conversation at the dinner table. Dad would ask me what was new, and I'd want to say something like, "Well I got a B-plus on my math test. We played softball in gym today. Scott's dying." In science class I wanted to ask what happens to people's bodies after they die. In casual conversations I found myself talking a lot about hospitals and blood and anesthetics. I started looking through the newspaper for pictures of car crashes, where you could see someone's arm or leg sticking out from under the wreckage.

But no matter what I was feeling inside, I had to make sure that nobody found out the truth. Especially Scott. So when I was feeling really sad, I made sure to act happy. When I was feeling angry, I'd try to look bored. When I was nervous, I'd act calm. When I was at home and just wanted to stay in my room all the time, I'd make sure to go out and talk to Mom or Dad and tell them how great things were going.

And the main thing I did was to try to see more and more of Scott. I didn't want him even to suspect that anything was wrong, so I tried to make him think that things were better than ever. Almost every day we were over at his house, listening to Joe Pyne or doing our homework or looking through the phone book for funny names. I decided that it was my job to see that Scott had a good time right up to the last. The trouble was, every time I smiled or joked around, it got harder to do. The more I pretended I was enjoying myself, the more tense I got.

I started to dread being with Scott. I'd get a wrenching feeling in my stomach whenever I saw him. It seemed that when I was with him, I'd always have either a stomachache or a headache. Anything could set it off—chess, the Big Five, talking about fruit flies. But to keep from letting him know that anything was wrong, I made sure to act the happiest when I hurt the most. Whenever I caught myself wanting to avoid him, I'd call him up and see if he wanted to do something.

Sometimes, when it got really bad, I'd write long letters and then throw them away. They always started out, "Dear world, Scott is dying."

[17]

I_t went on like that for two months. That's how long Scott was back at school. My headaches and my stomachaches got worse, but I think I did a pretty good job of covering them up and looking normal. The whole time, no one ever asked me what was wrong, not even Scott. Sometimes he'd glance at me in a funny way, but he never said anything.

It was just a week or so after Christmas vacation that Scott got sick again. This time I made sure to stop by his house after school. I didn't want him to get mad at me this time. I was hoping he was just having another one of those false alarms, like the time he was absent from school when he had the sniffles. But this was the real thing. I could tell by the look on Mrs. Lewis's face when she opened the door. She looked scared. Of course, she didn't want me to know.

"Oh, hi, Gary," she said, pretending to be cheerful.

"Hi, Mrs. Lewis. I just stopped by to say hello to Scott."

She swallowed hard. "I'm afraid Scott's not here, Gary. The doctor put him in the hospital to run some more tests. I guess it's that anemia again."

I tried to act nonchalant. "Do you think I could visit him?"

"Not—just yet. The doctor said he should get lots of rest this week. He said it would probably be best if Scott wasn't disturbed."

I wondered what the real reason was that the doctor didn't want Scott disturbed. How sick was he? For a minute I almost thought I was going to shout that question at Mrs. Lewis. But I didn't. I held it inside. I didn't want to upset anybody.

"Well, when you see Scott," I said in a normal voice, "tell him hello for me. Tell him I'm getting his homework assignments for him."

"I sure will," Mrs. Lewis replied. "And maybe you can visit him pretty soon. I'll check with the doctor."

"Thanks. I'd like that." I took a deep breath. "I guess I'd better get going. I have to get home. Mom's expecting me." Mom wasn't really expecting me, but I had to say something. I turned to go.

"It was nice of you to come by, Gary." I looked back at Mrs. Lewis. She seemed relieved now that I was going.

"Sure," I said, and hurried off.

I called the Lewises every few days to see if I could visit Scott. They kept telling me the same thing—the doctor was still running tests and didn't want Scott to be disturbed. They might as well have told me that Scott was trying out for the Olympics. I knew they were lying. In a way, though, I was glad when they told me I couldn't see him, because I was afraid of what he might look like.

But every time I was happy, it made me feel like a traitor to Scott, and then I felt awful.

Finally, after a week had gone by, I talked to Mrs. Lewis on the phone again, and she said I could visit Scott on Saturday. She also said that she and Mr. Lewis wanted to talk to me Friday night before I saw Scott, and so she invited me for dinner. She told me they would pick me up at six o'clock on Friday.

On Friday afternoon, everything went in slow motion. Walking home from school seemed to take hours. I tried to do some English homework, but my hand wouldn't write fast enough, and by the time I got halfway through a sentence, I'd forgotten how I wanted it to end. The same thing happened when I tried to read. The sentences were too long. The pages were too long. I read page 156 of my government textbook eight times. Finally, after what seemed like days, six o'clock arrived, and I heard a car pull up in front of the house. I grabbed my coat.

"They're here, Mom," I yelled. "See you later."

Mom appeared in the hallway. I wondered whether the Lewises had told her yet. I couldn't tell. She looked sad, but then she always looked sad.

"Be careful," she said. She said that a lot.

I walked out toward the Lewises' car. I could just barely see the top of Mr. Lewis's head over the steering wheel. He must have been slumped down again. Mrs. Lewis was beside him. I got in the front seat next to her, and we backed out of the driveway.

"Hey, I sure appreciate you inviting me over to dinner like this," I said real fast as we started down the street. "I usually just eat at home with Mom and Dad. I mean, not that there's anything wrong with that. I always enjoy being with them. Dad works, you know. I don't get to see him during the day. But then, even if he stayed home, I'd be at school, so we still couldn't see each other. It's too bad, you know, that families don't see more of each other. Dad says that's one of the problems with things today."

There was a pause. "We're glad you could make it tonight," Mr. Lewis said quietly. That's one thing I noticed about his voice that night. It was quieter than usual, almost muffled, as if he were talking through a handkerchief. "Mrs. Lewis made some roast beef," he said, "and we thought you might like to try it."

For the rest of the trip to their house and all through dinner, Mr. and Mrs. Lewis kept talking as if roast beef were the whole reason for inviting me over. Mrs. Lewis described how she cooked it, and Mr. Lewis told me how they always had it for special occasions. I didn't ask him what was so special about that night.

We discussed school and all the things I was doing. I could tell I was acting as strange as they were. I would either be really quiet, or I'd launch into a five-minute speech about English class or math or something, just like I'd done in the car. The less sense I was making, the faster I'd talk.

When we'd finished eating, I started to help take the dishes off the table like I did at home, but Mrs. Lewis stopped me.

"Let's go into the living room," she suggested. I got this chilly, tingly feeling in my chest.

[18]

Mr. Lewis motioned for me to sit on the couch. He and Mrs. Lewis sat in stuffed chairs opposite me. Everything was quiet for a minute. Then Mr. Lewis began.

"As you know, Gary, Scott's been sick," he said.

I spotted a bowl of M&Ms on the coffee table in front of me and reached for a handful.

"We've told you that he has anemia, but that's not quite true. Scott does have a blood disease, but it's not anemia. He has leukemia."

Mr. Lewis leaned forward. "There's no known cure for leukemia," he added. "It's a fatal disease." Mrs. Lewis shot him a withering glare.

I looked down at the M&Ms, and I popped a few into my mouth. They tasted pretty good. I'd always liked M&Ms. It wasn't true what they said on TV, though. They were melting in my hands.

When I looked up again, I noticed that Mrs. Lewis had

her face in her hands. She wasn't making any sound, but her shoulders were heaving up and down. She was sobbing.

"Hey, I'm sorry," I said quickly. I looked at Mr. Lewis. His jaw muscles were all tense, and he was just staring straight ahead. I began to worry that they might suspect I already knew.

I'd rehearsed this moment a hundred times in my mind, but now that it had come, I blew it. Instead of sounding grave and shocked and concerned, it all came tumbling out in an unconvincing rush: "That's terrible news. Leukemia, huh? That's awful. I never would have guessed it in a million years. I just thought it was anemia. I figured as soon as they took a few more tests, he'd be out of the hospital and back at school. Leukemia. Wow."

Mr. Lewis looked over at his wife and then back at me. "Of course," he went on, "we don't know how long it will take for Scott to—for the disease to run it course. The doctor says that usually it's either very quick, or else it takes quite a long time—maybe even years. I guess our hope is that Scott will live long enough for them to develop a cure for leukemia." He lapsed into silence again. Mrs. Lewis was wiping her eyes with some Kleenex.

I took another handful of M&Ms and put a few in my mouth. I chewed them, and as I was swallowing, they got caught in my throat or something, because I started coughing like a madman. It was the kind of cough where your face gets red, and you think you'll never be able to breathe again.

Mr. Lewis rushed over and grabbed me and started pounding me on the back. Mrs. Lewis went into the kitchen and got me a glass of water, and then she put her arm around my shoulders and pushed my hair up out of my face. I couldn't believe how concerned they were acting. It was as if they had been just waiting for an excuse to stop talking and start doing something helpful for somebody. And then I got the strangest feeling as I was sitting there coughing, with the Lewises on each side of me. I got the feeling I was Scott. Here they were, acting as if I were dying or something, and all that had happened was that I'd swallowed an M&M the wrong way.

I kept drinking water and clearing my throat, and pretty soon the coughing stopped. Mr. and Mrs. Lewis went back to their chairs. I felt embarrassed, as if I'd been trying to steal the stage from Scott.

"There's one more thing we should tell you," Mrs. Lewis said. "We've decided not to say anything about this to Scott. It's too big a burden for a thirteen-year-old boy."

That was my chance. I should have yelled, "Too big a burden! Scott's the one who's dying. If anybody has the right to know, he does! You can't keep it from him! It's not fair!"

"I guess you're right," I said out loud.

"When you see Scott tomorrow," Mrs. Lewis went on, "just try to act as though everything were normal. He still thinks he has anemia. Don't tell him the truth."

Mr. Lewis leaned forward. "Gary, try not to be shocked by the way Scott looks. Frankly, he doesn't look very good." He laced his fingers together and clenched his hands tight. "I guess that's the reason we decided to tell you about . . . Scott's condition. You would have wondered when you saw him."

"We didn't want you to ask him any awkward questions," Mrs. Lewis added quickly.

I shouldn't have let that go past. I should have stood up right then and shouted, "Awkward questions? Is it awkward to ask somebody what's really wrong with him? Is it impolite to ask a person why he looks sick? When somebody's dying, who cares about being polite?"

"I wouldn't want to upset him," I said out loud. "Don't worry about me. I'll just act perfectly normal."

"We've told your parents, too," said Mrs. Lewis. "I guess it's no big secret anymore. Just as long as Scott doesn't find out."

"How long have you known about this?" I asked them.

"Ever since Scott went to the hospital for the first time," Mr. Lewis replied. "They ran some tests that showed it. We told Scott's teachers about it so they'd understand his absences, but they were the only ones who knew."

"Boy," I said, shaking my head, "I would never have known. You really kept it a secret."

Mrs. Lewis reached over and touched my arm. "I'm just sorry we had to tell you now."

I was starting to feel funny. "I think I'd better get going," I said. I couldn't think of anything else to say.

Mr. Lewis got up from his chair. "I'll take you home," he offered, and shuffled across the living room to the coat closet.

I turned to Mrs. Lewis. "I sure enjoyed that roast beef," I said.

When I walked in the door of my house, I saw Mom and Dad sitting together on the couch in the living room. Mom had her hands pressed flat on her lap, and Dad had his arm around her. I figured they were watching TV, but as I moved into the room, I realized the TV was off. They looked up when they heard me.

"Mrs. Lewis called and told me this afternoon," Mom said in a shaky voice. "Your father and I are very sorry about this."

I just kept moving in the direction of my room.

"You know, son," Dad said behind me, "the ball game's never over till the last out."

I went into my room and shut the door. It seemed that I had been spending a lot of time there recently. I sat on the edge of the bed.

So now it was official. I knew that Scott was dying. I decided that this was probably a good time to cry. I tried thinking of Scott in pain. I tried thinking of him with enlarged lymph glands, bleeding easily, as it said in the encyclopedia. I tried thinking of Mr. and Mrs. Lewis eating dinner alone, with Scott's place empty. I tried thinking what it would be like for me after Scott was gone. I tried thinking all the sad thoughts I could, but nothing seemed to take. I finally tried pinching myself really hard.

I couldn't even get my lip to tremble.

[19]

Mom drove me to the hospital the next morning. About halfway there, I happened to notice a vase of flowers in the back seat.

"What are those for?" I asked.

"They're for Scott. I thought he might like them."

For some reason, the thought of flowers in Scott's room made me angry. "Scott doesn't like flowers," I protested. "You're not taking those into his room."

Mom was quiet for a minute, and then in a low voice she said, "Gary, you're only thirteen years old. You've never had to stay in a hospital. You have no idea what it's like. Flowers are always welcome in a hospital room."

Ordinarily I would have said something back to her, but her voice had an odd, determined sound that took me by surprise, and so I kept quiet.

Scott was in a different room this time, but even so we found it a lot quicker than the last time. As I walked through the door with Mom behind me, for some reason I looked at everything else before I looked at Scott.

In the bed to the far left was a boy about five years old with a big white cast on one leg. He was sitting up in bed, and some people were gathered around talking to him. It was probably his parents and grandparents. They had brought him some toys and things, and they were all chattering away about something or other.

In the bed straight ahead was a rugged-looking older man with dark-brown, wrinkled skin like you get when you're out in the sun a lot. The thing I noticed right away was this long scar across one cheek. He almost looked like one of those guys you see in cigarette ads with tattoos on their arms. He was watching a football game on TV.

Over to the right was Scott's area. I say "Scott's area" because Scott himself wasn't there. The bed was empty. It was all messed up, as if he had just been in it, but there was no one there. The reason you could tell it was Scott's area was because of all the things around the bed. There were issues of *Scientific American* on the nightstand, a chessboard on a nearby chair, a book about folk music next to the pillow, and on the walls around the bed, three *National Geographic* posters about different things in the world of science. One of them had a close-up picture of a fruit fly.

With all of this stuff scattered around, and with people visiting and watching TV in the background, the place seemed pretty comfortable. It was almost homey. I started feeling a lot better. Until Scott stepped into the room.

Scott looked like an old man. He was hunched over, as if he didn't have the energy to stand up straight. His hair was getting thin, and bald patches showed through. The skin on his arms was almost as white as the linoleum floor.

To complete the picture, his hospital gown was all wrinkled, and he had on a ratty-looking pair of slippers—the kind they wear in old people's homes.

He had been in the bathroom. When he first stepped back into the room, he didn't notice Mom and me right away.

"How are you doing, Scott?" I ventured.

He looked up groggily, and I saw his face for the first time. I guess he said hi, but I didn't hear him. I was too busy staring at his eyes.

I saw a science-fiction movie a few years ago that scared me to death. It was about a town that was being invaded by Martians. But the Martians didn't invade from outside in a flying saucer. They invaded from the inside, taking over people's bodies one by one. When someone was taken over, he looked just the same, except for his eyes. They were bright red. Those bright-red eyes really shook me up.

That's what I thought of when I saw Scott, because his eyes were bright red. When I say bright red, I don't mean the part in the middle, which is always colored. I mean the part that's usually white. The whites of his eyes had turned the color of blood.

I guess I never realized before how important a person's eyes are. When you look at them, you can tell a lot about the way a person is feeling. Sometimes they kind of sparkle. Sometimes they're deep and sad. Sometimes they're shifty. But with Scott, you couldn't tell anything. All you could see was the color of blood. His eyes were so red that it almost looked as if there were no eyes there at all. Only empty sockets.

Then I looked at the rest of his face. It didn't look much better. There were red spots all over it, especially on his nose and cheeks. Over one of his eyes was a bruise, and there were other bruises on his neck. It sounds terrible, but looking at him made me sick to my stomach. I tried not to show it, though.

Scott sat down on the edge of the bed. I smiled and tried to keep from staring at him too much. Mom took a couple of nervous steps forward and set the vase of flowers on the table next to him.

"Here's something to brighten up the room," Mom said. "I just wanted you to know we were thinking of you."

There was still something about having those flowers in Scott's room that made me feel funny. I guess maybe it reminded me of a church or a graveyard or something. I waited to see what Scott would do.

He looked at her and smiled a weak smile. "Thanks, Mrs. Matthews," he said. "That's really nice."

So he didn't just look strange; he was acting strange, too. Scott wouldn't usually say something like that—especially when people did things like giving him flowers.

Mom went over and sat down in a chair by the door, and I settled into a visitors' chair right by the bed. Scott got back in bed, still moving slowly, and sat with a pillow propping him up. No one said anything for a few minutes. All I could think of to say was, "Scott, you look terrible." It kept running through my head, and I was worried that if I spoke too quickly, it might pop out.

I looked around the room, doing my best to act casual while I tried to figure out some way of starting a conversation. The longer it took, the more nervous I got.

Finally, in desperation, I blurted out, "Nice room you got here."

Scott looked at me. "Thanks," he said. He didn't say anything else, and we lapsed into silence again.

I guess the usual thing you'd expect to talk about with a

hospital patient would be how he was feeling. But that was a subject I didn't want to bring up. I knew how it was going to turn out, and that was as much as I wanted to know—more than I wanted to know. Any daily or weekly reports on how he was doing could only cloud the issue. So I figured it was best to avoid the subject. I guess Scott figured the same thing, for whatever reason, because he never brought the subject up during that visit. Instead, we ended up talking about other things.

"School's kind of dull these days," I said finally.

"I'll trade places with you any day," Scott replied. "At least you get to move around. I have to stay in this stupid bed all the time. Have you ever had to lie in bed for a whole week? Your butt gets sore. You get tired of looking at the same old things. The room seems smaller every day. Those white walls start closing in on you. I'd give anything to be out in a field someplace."

He was talking about the hospital as though he were there because of some mistake, as if he were just as healthy as I was. I felt like holding up a mirror in front of him so he could see how he looked. Whom was he kidding? He fit right in. Where else would you put a thirteen-year-old kid who walks like an old man and looks like a Martian? The reason Scott was in a hospital and I was in school was because he was sick and I was healthy. He was dying. I wasn't.

"Let's play some chess," I suggested. I didn't really feel that much like playing, but I didn't want to talk anymore. I was afraid I might say something I shouldn't.

About halfway through the game, a nurse came in and interrupted us.

"It's that time again," she announced in a perky voice. She had a glass of water and a handful of pills. There were six or seven of them, and she had Scott swallow every last one.

When he finished, she glanced at me and back at Scott.

"I see you've got visitors today," she said, smiling. And then, just for a second, a sad look flickered across her eyes. It occurred to me that she must know, too. Everyone knew but Scott.

"You look awfully tired," she said to him. "Why don't you two finish up the game, and then maybe your friend should be going."

Scott nodded, and we turned back to our game. It was over in no time, because I wasn't really trying. Scott had me in checkmate before I even noticed. I just didn't have my heart in it. I guess playing chess was better than talking, but it wasn't exactly what I wanted to do at that moment. What I wanted to do was leave. I was glad the nurse had suggested it, because I wouldn't have known how to bring it up. I would probably have just stayed there until somebody had said something. I would never have wanted Scott to think I didn't like visiting him.

I helped Scott put the chessboard back on the nightstand, and then I stood up to go. I tried not to look anxious to leave.

"It was sure good to see you again, Scott," I mouthed. "I hope you're feeling better."

"When are you coming back?"

"Soon," I said, not wanting to think about it. "Probably in a couple of days."

"Maybe you can stay longer next time," he said. "I'll try to save up my energy." He smiled a wobbly smile.

Mom came over and stood next to me.

"We'll be thinking about you, Scott," she said.

"Thanks again for the flowers, Mrs. Matthews," Scott

blurted out. "It was sure nice of you to bring them." He was starting to sound desperate, almost as if he couldn't stand to see us go. It was pathetic. I had to get out of there.

"See you again soon," I said quickly. I grabbed Mom's arm, turned her around, and we walked toward the door. I think I sort of waved as we left the room.

[20]

I_t would have been simple for me to go visit Scott a few days later, say Monday or Tuesday. I'm sure Mom would have taken me, and I think Mrs. Lewis would have let me go with her if I'd asked. It also would have been simple for me to call Scott on the phone. In fact, I could have done that every day. I could have let him know how things were going at school, or we could have just talked about movies or science or politics or folk music. Anything, really. You know how it is when you're sick and cooped up all day in one place. You're glad to talk to anybody—especially your best friend. But I didn't visit him or call him all that week. Or the next.

At first I told myself that he was probably too sick to see or talk to anybody. That worked for a few days. Then I decided I was getting behind in my homework and should spend all my time catching up. I kept telling myself that as soon as I finished it, I'd go see Scott. By finishing my homework, I wouldn't have anything hanging over my head when I was talking to him. That worked for another three or four days. After that, I couldn't think of any reason why I shouldn't see Scott, and so I just tried not to think about it. That worked off and on. When it was working, I was okay. I was pretty much my normal self, except maybe a little quieter than usual. When it wasn't working, I didn't do too well.

One thing I really hate is headaches, especially those really bad ones, when your whole head is throbbing and you start feeling sick to your stomach. I got some of those headaches at school during those two weeks. Ordinarily I would have asked to go to the nurse's office so I could lie down until the aching went away. But I didn't want anybody to think anything was wrong. So the more my head hurt, the more I tried to act as if I'd never felt better in my life. That way, no one would ask me any questions about what was bothering me.

Saturday morning after the second week, I was helping Mom hang some pictures. A couple of times she tried to bring up the subject of Scott. I just pretended I didn't hear her, and after a while she stopped trying. We weren't saying much of anything. Just about the only noise was an occasional tack being driven into the wall.

Then the phone rang. In the quiet house, it sounded like a fire alarm. I reached over and picked up the receiver.

"Hello."

"Gary, this is Mrs. Lewis."

Suddenly I got this really tight feeling in my chest. My two weeks of avoiding Scott loomed up in front of me. Now Mrs. Lewis would probably ask me to go visit him again.

"Hi, Mrs. Lewis," I said, trying to sound normal. "How are things going?"

"Gary," she said, "Scott passed away last night. I thought you'd want to know."

I just stood there for a minute, staring straight ahead.

"He'd been getting steadily worse for the past couple of weeks," she went on, "and finally the complications got the better of him. It happened last night about ten."

My lips were moving, but nothing was coming out. I could feel the air building up into a huge bubble in my chest. Finally I broke through.

"But that can't be," I said breathlessly. "I was going to come visit him. I was going to tell him all about school. We could have played some more chess. We could have talked about Woody Guthrie and *Scientific American*. I figured there was plenty of time."

"Well," she said in this low, sad voice, "I guess he went more quickly than any of us expected."

"Yeah, but at least you were there with him when it happened. I was at home watching TV, drinking a Coke or something."

Now her voice was even quieter. "Maybe it's just as well," she said. "He—didn't look very good toward the end."

That sort of took the steam out of me. I got this sudden picture of Scott with bruises and big red splotches all over his face and arms. And those dark-red eyes. I didn't feel like talking anymore.

Then I noticed that the room was quiet and that Mom was standing just a few feet away, looking at me with this pinched expression on her face.

I turned back to the phone. "You want to talk to Mom?" I asked Mrs. Lewis.

"All right," she replied. "And, Gary—don't be so hard on yourself. Scott enjoyed seeing you that last time. He told me that again and again."

"Yeah," I mumbled. I handed the receiver to Mom. She took it with the tips of her fingers, as if it were a dead cat.

I stumbled across the living room and back to my bedroom, pushing the door shut behind me. I eased myself down onto the bed and just lay there on my stomach, with my arms crossed under my chin.

Scott was dead. I'd never see him again. I'd had two weeks to visit him again and I'd blown it. I could have gone yesterday, or the day before, or the day before that. I should have gone every day. I was supposed to be his best friend. I should have been over there constantly, cheering him up and making him feel better. But instead, I was too busy doing my homework and acting as if nothing were wrong. I'd tried not to think about him, even. I'd pretended that Scott Lewis didn't even exist, let alone that he was my best friend and was in the hospital. And now he was dead. Mrs. Lewis had said "passed away," but "dead" was really the only word for it. Now all that was left of Scott was a body, lying somewhere in the basement of the hospital. In the morgue. Just like those fruit flies.

There was a knock at my door. I knew it was Mom. I didn't want to talk to her. I was afraid she'd say something about Jesus. So I just lay there, quiet.

She knocked again. "Gary," she said, "I just want to talk to you." I still didn't say anything. I didn't even face toward the door.

There was another knock. "Gary, are you all right? Are you in there? Gary?" Her voice was getting shriller.

"Gary, if you're in there, say something. Say something to me! Gary? Gary?"

Suddenly, I could hear the door swing open. There was a pause, then, "Oh, Gary, I—"

"Get out of my room," I interrupted, not even turning around. I heard her take a quick breath. Then there was silence.

"I'm sorry," she said finally in a tiny voice.

I heard her leave the room and click the door shut behind her.

[21]

Scott's funeral was Monday afternoon. I didn't go to school that day. I didn't even get up. It would have meant having to talk to people, and there was no one I wanted to talk to. When my alarm went off, I just shut it off and turned over. Usually if I did that, Dad would come pounding on my door a few minutes later to make sure I was up. But that morning no one bothered me.

Around noon I came out of my room. Mom started to say something, but I just stared right past her, and she kept quiet. I walked straight into the kitchen, fixed myself a sandwich, walked straight back to my room, and shut the door behind me.

Later that afternoon, I got ready for the funeral. I put on my Sunday school clothes, with the itchy wool pants and the stiff white collar.

Mom and I drove up to the mortuary and waited out in

front of the chapel for Dad. While we waited, I didn't feel like saying anything, so I just watched the people go inside. I didn't know most of them, except for Mrs. McNeill. When I saw her coming down the sidewalk, I turned my back. I guess she didn't see me.

When Dad got there, the three of us walked through the doors of the chapel. I expected organ music. Instead, they were playing one of Scott's folk-music records. Woody Guthrie was singing. The record had that same scratchy sound it had when Scott used to play it on his beat-up record player. I started blinking my eyes and breathing real fast.

I tried to concentrate on what I was doing. I clenched my fists and looked right at Mom's back as I followed her and Dad up the aisle to our seats. When we sat down, Mom went to pat my shoulder, and I brushed her hand away. I didn't want anyone touching me or talking to me. I felt like on a tightrope. I couldn't breathe too deeply or move too quickly or look off to the side or think about what was down below. I just had to stare at my folded hands and concentrate on them as hard as I could—just take one step at a time and get through it all without slipping or losing control. I didn't want to lose control. I had to concentrate. And that music wasn't helping any.

The song went on and on, and then finally it faded away and the organ music started. I shifted in my seat a little bit and decided to look up. There, right up in front, at the head of the aisle, was the casket. My stomach tightened. I couldn't take my eyes off that casket. People call them caskets, but if you really look at one, you can see that it's just a wooden box. The wooden box was closed, and inside was Scott.

He was actually right inside of it. I couldn't see him, but

I knew he was there. I tried to imagine what it was like in that box. Probably cold and hard. Probably dark. I shivered and had to look away.

People said afterward that the service was short. It seemed long to me. I couldn't wait for it to end. First there was that folk music, then the organ music, and then the sermon. The man who preached it was a minister at the Unitarian church where Mrs. Lewis went sometimes. As far as I know, Scott had never gone there, so I couldn't see where this minister got the right to talk about Scott at his funeral. He thought he knew all about Scott. He described the kind of person Scott was, saying how he wanted to help the poor people of the world and was compassionate and tender and loving. You'd think Scott had been Jesus or something. It was sickening. The minister didn't even know Scott. He hadn't been his friend. I felt like shouting out, "When was the last time you saw him?" Then I realized that if the minister had ever gone with Mrs. Lewis to the hospital, there was a good chance he'd seen Scott more recently than I had. So who was I to talk? If I knew Scott so well, where had I been the last two weeks? Why couldn't I have taken five lousy minutes to give Scott a call and let him know I was still his friend?

At the end of the sermon, the minister asked if there was anyone in the audience who wanted to say something more about Scott. There was a long silence. People looked around at each other. I felt Mom look over at me, and some other people did, too. I felt my face get hot. It seemed that everybody wanted me to say something, but I wasn't going to. I had had my chance to talk—to Scott, not to a bunch of strangers—and I had missed it. Now it was too late. Now I just had to shut up and pay the price.

My face got hotter and hotter, but I didn't say anything. I just stared down at my hands.

When no one volunteered, the minister stepped out from behind the pulpit and walked over to the casket. I figured he was going to say a prayer or something. Instead, he lifted the lid and invited everyone to come up, row by row, and get one last look at Scott.

I could hardly believe it. No one had told me about this. I had figured they'd just bury the box and that would be it. I sure wasn't going to go look at Scott. I'd just walk right past the casket and go out the side door. But then, as we waited for the first few rows to file to the front, I started getting curious. I'd never seen a dead person before. I wondered what they looked like. I wondered what Scott looked like. The last time I'd seen him, he had looked terrible. I wanted to see if he looked any different when he died.

When they got to our row, I still hadn't made up my mind for sure. I walked slowly up the aisle, still trying to decide, feeling all knotted up inside. The casket looked bigger every minute. I had to decide pretty soon. As we reached the head of the aisle, I suddenly took a few quick steps over to the casket and looked down inside.

I was prepared for Scott to look ugly and splotched and discolored. I wasn't prepared for him to look pretty. They had dressed him up in his nicest clothes, all pressed and clean. He had powder on his face and rouge on his cheeks. There was some lipstick, too. Even his fingernails had been manicured. He didn't look like Scott. He didn't look real.

I had to get out. I ran toward the side door, bumping into a man and almost knocking him over and then pushing some other people aside. I lurched through the door and past the people waiting on the lawn. There was a big tree nearby. I stumbled over there and leaned against it, out of control now. I was sobbing, with my head in my folded arms. I could feel my whole body shaking, and I couldn't stop it. All I could think of was that dressed-up doll in the box. The real Scott was gone. The Scott who played chess and scared B7s and read *Playboy* was gone. And I hadn't even said good-bye.

The rest of the afternoon all blended together. I remember walking with everyone up the hill to the place where Scott was going to be buried. I remember how they lowered the wooden box into the ground. I remember choosing to ride home in the back seat of the car instead of in the front, between Mom and Dad, where I usually sat. I remember watching TV all evening in my wool pants and stiff collar, not wanting to change clothes. Mostly, though, I remember feeling that somehow all the sadness and all the pain were my fault. And I guess I still feel that way.

Epilogue

It's been over a year now since Scott died. I haven't talked to anyone about it—not even my parents. People keep asking me if I want to discuss it, and I say no. But it still bothers me. I can't seem to shake it.

After Scott died, Mom talked a lot about eternal life and how people live on forever after they die. I don't believe in the kind of eternal life she meant, but I read somewhere about another kind of eternal life. It's when people remember you. As long as your friends keep thinking about you and remember what you were like, you're still alive in a way. You're only dead when people stop thinking about you. That made sense to me. It wasn't the same as Mom's eternal life, but it was better than nothing.

So I started making a special point of thinking about Scott as much as I could. I'd try to picture him in my mind and remember his freckles and his big hands and the way he used to laugh and slap his leg. I'd try to remember the different things he said and the different expressions he would get on his face. Whatever I was doing, I'd always try to think of Scott as much as I could. That's what friends are for, isn't it?

But after a few weeks I noticed it was harder to do. I'd get involved in something, and before you knew it, I wouldn't be thinking about Scott at all. Sometimes I'd go for as long as an hour like that. Then my mind would snap back to Scott, and I'd feel terrible—as if I had let him down all over again.

So I tried harder. But then another problem came up. Every once in a while, I had trouble remembering what he looked like. Instead of seeing him the way he really looked, I'd picture him in the hospital looking like an old man, or in that casket looking like a store dummy. I'd shake my head and try again, but sometimes I just couldn't remember. So I got out a color snapshot I had of Scott and put it next to the window in my bedroom. It showed Scott at the beach, playing his guitar. He was leaning over, looking down at the strings, with his tongue poking out of the corner of his mouth, trying to get the fingerings right. It wasn't what you'd call a flattering picture, but it really looked like Scott. Whenever I had trouble remembering what he looked like, I'd go into my bedroom and stare at that picture for a while.

But recently I've noticed something. The picture is fading—not much, but just enough so you can tell it's getting lighter. It must be the sun coming in the window that's doing it. Whatever it is, Scott is slowly fading away. In a year or two, there'll probably only be some dim outlines left, and then after that, nothing at all. That really scares me. I always thought that pictures lasted forever.

Sometimes I get mad at Scott. Sometimes I feel that all this is his fault. After all, I didn't ask for it to happen. It wasn't my idea. He's the one who got sick. He's the one who died. I know it sounds crazy, but that's what I think sometimes. And then as soon as I think it, I feel terrible again. Some friend. I run out on Scott, I leave him there to die, and then I blame everything on him. Some friend. Some great friend.

I know what's going to happen now. I'm going to feel bad for a while longer, maybe a few months, maybe a few years. Then gradually it's all going to fade away, just like that picture. Whatever was left of Scott inside of me will be gone.

I don't understand how someone can just fade away. I don't understand why Scott died. I don't understand why I let him down. I thought we were friends.